DEVITA DURAN

GETS STONED

Mark Spector

ISBN: 979-8-9992054-1-4
Cover Art: Shutterstock
Cover Design: Mark Spector

Printed on Demand

Dedicated to the 20-something dreamer who wanted to write comic science fiction, but instead bet (successfully) on an advertising career.

You never could have pulled this off.

DEVITA DURAN

GETS STONED

DONLAN'S

Oh My Damn ItNess! How could Donlon's be so quiet?

Middle of happy hour, wall-to-wall corp. dorks and dorkesses—the joint should have been rollicking like hyenas on nitrous, the bar-breath air teeming with gossip about adulterous bosses, mockery of stupid clients, and braying over nickels of arbitrage.

But tonight, nothing. Just somber whispers on a soundtrack of nursing-home folk-pop.

One voice rose above the hushed mumbles. Some carrot-topped creep with a Fu Manchu mustache was hitting on a blond, talking her implants off about dung beetle mating rituals, and I heard every word from half a bar's length away.

Not the best environment for my upcoming conversation.

My name is Devita Duran, and on this night, I was still the hottest mood mistress in New York. People hired me like they hired disc jockeys in the last century. But while those characters used music to amp up parties, my methods were more subtle, effective, and illegal. I got under everybody's skin with ultra-fine mists of psychoactive drugs, most of which I invented myself.

My old bosses, Klecko and Cal, were waiting for me at a booth near the front of the bar. They'd gotten richer than rich off my formula for Duplextacy. Now I wanted to cut them in for a piece of my newest psychopharmacological masterpiece, 6S.

But if Creepo Manchuo's fetishy gush about shit balls and dung-top dancing could reach me from this distance, any straight-assed suit in this crowd could catch snippets of our meeting, and details of the partnership I hoped to launch. Nothing we were about to discuss was legal.

I'd chosen Donlon's for this meeting because the acoustics create a soundproof bubble around each booth. But only when the bar is loud. I needed more volume. Not easy without my misting machines and chemicals.

Fortunately, there's more than one way to start a party, and I had many tools to work with.

I slithered through the crowd to the jukebox, cuing my wristwatch on the way.

Ha! Five years ago, none of these profit mongers would hire me out of college, and now, I had more money than any of them. And skills. I slapped my watch on the jukebox and activated my hack. Goodbye, bedpan music. The next song would kick off a long set of loud, distracting funk.

I turned around and—Oh My UprightNess!—there stood Bick Johnstone, the green screener with the joystick *Idolatry Ezine* had anointed, "Hottest Plunger on the Planet." No wonder that blond stood for that creep's shit. She was looking right past his sleazy mustache to the boldest bulge in the bar.

And she wasn't alone. Every girl in Donlon's cast at least the occasional eye in Bick Johnstone's direction. Some openly gawked. They all wanted him.

But, and I say this in all modesty, no girl in this bar was any match for Devita Duran.

My soft, flowing, shoulder-length brown hair frames a face that Helen of Troy would envy. Big, almond-shaped blue eyes. High, sculpted cheekbones with a little pink, figure-eight beauty mark below my right eye. A straight, refined nose. And soft, honey rose lips that fit my well-defined jawline.

Better still, my magnificent face sits atop a busty yet skinny *Meme Girl of the Century* bod. A red bodysuit and tight blue jeans, both form-fitted, accentuated my figure's many highlights.

I was going to mount the Bick Johnstone trophy. I could feel it in my—

I'll spare you the quivering details.

When the first big bass note of funk-a-loudness hit, I raised my arms. Hands up, boobs out, I danced through the crowded lane between the bar and the booths.

With moves calibrated to wake the crowd, I made sure to move toward Bick Johnstone. I wanted to catch his eye. Make him notice me. Then, just before I reached him, I'd slip into my meeting with Klecko and Cal and leave him to wonder what I was up to.

If I was right—and when am I ever wrong with guys?—thoughts about me would distract him from other girls. He'd remember my face and bod. Then, when my meeting was over, I'd move in for the kill.

Devita Duran knows how to make out and make business.

I shook everything I had. Really shook it. I twirled left. I spun right. I bent down. I sprung up. Twirling left and spinning right. Bending down and springing up—right into a tangly mess of burnt-orange chest hair, rusty steel wool protruding from an open-past-the-man-boobs black shirt.

Blinded by my hair waving across my face, I hadn't seen Creepo Manchuo step into my path.

I withdrew in horror. His smug grin would have looked at home on a cartoon canine, especially with the ends of that mustache curled up toward his eyes. Gobs of gel kept a frizzy orange mop glued to his head. He exuded that noxious odor of beery sweat and spoke with slow, sticky enunciations that slimed their way into my brain.

"How can I get you to have a drink with me?" he said.

"Serve booze at your wake," I replied.

Then, just to make him want me, I flashed my classic Devita Duran tease-of-a-wink. I like to mess with guys' heads.

I twirled past him and danced to the front of the bar. When I got to Klecko and Cal's booth, I stopped.

My moves worked. The voices around the bar were louder, the music funkier. Bass beats from the seatback speakers collided with the bar's din, bubbling the table in an audio shell. Klecko, Cal, and I could hear each other, but nobody could hear us.

I looked back toward Bick Johnstone. Creepo Manchuo's blond was now monopolizing his attention. But the night was young. There'd be plenty of time to move in after my meeting.

I pulled up the 6S app on my watch and tuned it to 1:00. Just enough for an edge. With a deep breath to capture confidence, I smiled and slid into the booth across from my old bosses.

KLECKO AND CAL

Klecko greeted me with a familiar, noncommittal smile. "Nice boob job," he said.

"It's all me," I replied.

Yes! Familiar banter. Klecko only joked when he was in a good mood.

Klecko was a tall, muscle-bound, bouncer type with a SWAT-team neck and a hard, square jaw. A black tee shirt clung to his torso. His thick, solid arms sported a new set of snake tattoos. I thought of complimenting the artistry but realized 6S might be showing me an illusion.

Cal was smaller and thinner than his partner. As usual, he started the meeting hiding his hands below the table. His greasy black hair and pockmarked face gave him the look of a sly nerd. A fox in a sheep suit. His pointy ears, a 6S illusion for sure, stood straight and alert. His eyes seemed more cunning and perceptive than usual.

Cal chimed in, "Yeah, you were always the hottie. Our golden goose of a…"

He stopped before he could say, "mood mistress."

The boobless, little titmouse of a waitress leaned into our table, puncturing the sound bubble. She put down two beers for Klecko and Cal and, for me, a Sex on the Beach—double vodka. Yogi, the big bear of a bartender, knows what I like when I talk business.

Klecko lifted his beer stein to his lips. Cal brought his three-fingered hands to the table and wrapped them around his beer. Each finger looked like a bent, knobby limb on a sick tree.

Cal never told anyone how he'd lost his thumbs and pinkies, nor how the other fingers got so smashed, but the injury never held him back. Cal could appear more dexterous with three deformed fingers than a concert pianist with five good ones.

If you saw Klecko and Cal together, you'd figure Cal for the business half of the team and Klecko for the doer and enforcer. And you'd be right. Sort of. It would be a mistake to underestimate Klecko's brains or Cal's strength.

When I graduated college into a world where too many STEMers chased too few jobs, they got me into mood misting.

Count on bad guys to give you a break when good guys won't.

The waitress left; we could speak softly and freely. The music, boisterous and loud throughout the bar, faded to ambience in the booth.

"Our clients loved you," Cal said. "Your moves got parties hopping before the first spray hit the air."

"Of course, your clients loved me," I said. "Anyone can drop chemicals into a mood mister. But when I toss my assets and smile into the mix, dancing around the room and tweaking the sprays, everybody has a good time and leaves happy."

Cal nodded without a smile or change to his expression. "From what I hear, you're still using those tricks. Are you really pulling enough cash for a fortieth-floor corner apartment?"

"And a lab here in Midtown," I added.

"Not bad," said Cal.

"Yes," I said. "When you got a formula that works, you stick with it."

"Like the formulas you stole from us," interjected Klecko.

I didn't expect that. "The only formulas I took are the ones I came up with," I countered. "You didn't want them."

"Klecko, drop it," Cal said. "We let her take a shot. Devita wanted to turn mood misting into an art, and we had no interest."

"My motto was, 'Work the crowd, not the chemicals.' You thought I was crazy."

14

Cal nodded. "We considered your ideas, but they didn't fit our business plan."

"So, you let me go on my own, thinking I would fail."

Cal raised an eyebrow and hardened his stare, a reminder that they hadn't exactly let me go.

Before I joined Klecko and Cal, they would spread misting machines around a room, load them with happy chemicals, and leave. I re-engineered the misters to hold multiple chemicals and deliver timed, mixed sprays. I also created inhibitors so the psychoactive mists wouldn't affect me. That let me stay at parties and orchestrate moods, start to finish. Revelers at a Devita Duran event experienced wild swings from calm and joy to exuberance and wild abandon. They always went home blissfully content.

Klecko and Cal's mood misting business doubled, but when I told them what I was doing, they told me to stop. They could have expanded into concerts, rallies, and—what is now my newest venture—persistent atmospheres. No imagination.

Eventually, they agreed to give me three months to test my ideas, but I knew I wasn't going back. By the time those three months were up, all their customers, as I expected, were calling me. In an underworld business, that could be suicide. Unless I left them with something more valuable than the business I took: the recipe for a street drug called Duplextacy. They could build a network to sell it; I couldn't. It was now the best-selling high in Amerika, and they had a monopoly. Nobody could crack Duplextacy's chemical formula or replicate the recipe I gave them.

But now, in this conversation, Klecko and Cal showed no interest in acknowledging the money my invention was making them. "You were supposed to call us after three months," said Cal.

"We agreed to talk," I countered. "You could have called me. But from what I understand, mood misting would have been a distraction. Your Duplextacy business was taking off, and you were making buckets of money on my formula."

"Not exactly your formula," Klecko interjected. "We modified it."

"I wouldn't call it a modification," said Cal. "More of a tweak."

Klecko argued, "But that tweak made it the big seller it became."

Cal nodded. He and Klecko never stopped looking at me while they staged their little tiff. Never lifted their beers.

I got the message: they thought they, not I, had made Duplextacy the hottest high on the street.

But I wasn't buying. They knew Duplextacy's effect on their customers and how to make it, but I had never shared with them the underlying chemical composition or how the drug worked its magic. What tweak could they make to a formula they didn't know or understand?

"And now, here we are, two years later," Cal said, "and you're still in business for yourself, and your mood mistressing keeps getting better. I hear you can turn a church service into an orgy."

"I only did that once. Practical joker paid a fortune for it."

"That fortune should have been ours," Klecko interjected. "That joker was our customer, not yours."

"That's on you, not me," I said. "Your mood misting business grew on the back of my formulas and engineering. When I left, I only took the inventions you didn't want. It's not my fault your customers didn't want the ones you kept."

Cal nodded. Klecko hardened his stare.

"Do you honestly think your tweak made Duplextacy into a bestseller? What did you do? Make my orange pills purple? You don't know the chemistry. All you have is the recipe I gave you. Without it, you'd have nothing to tweak. If this was another business, I could sue you for royalties."

The snake tattoos on Klecko's arm writhed. He was getting angry. "Royalties?"

"Calm down, you two," said Cal. "We're not here to talk about the past. It's time to move on. Devita says she has a proposition. Let's hear her out." Cal talked to the two of us, but the intensity in his eyes stayed focused on me.

Maybe this meeting was a mistake.

I swigged my drink.

"Look, you guys gave me my break," I acceded. "I appreciate that. Both of our businesses have grown since I left. But I still do more

16

research and development than you, and I have something that I think can be bigger than Duplextacy. I call it 6S."

Klecko chuckled. "6S, huh?" He turned to Cal. "Do you think Devita's stoned on 6S right now?"

Cal shifted his eyes to study my face, shoulders, body, arms, and hands. "Maybe. Hard to tell. She looks a little high, but I never knew Devita to take any drug except to test. She wouldn't take 6S and sit here without an inhibitor in her system or an antidote nearby."

Klecko cracked a grin. "She looks a little high to me."

"You're both right," I said. "I'm high on 6S, but only a little. I also have an inhibitor. 6S is an adjustable high. Customers can turn it on and off and up and down."

Cal nodded. "Tell us more."

Klecko's tats calmed down. Maybe this meeting would yield a deal after all.

"6S lives in the brain for five years," I explained. "But it's dormant until you activate it. After you turn it on, 6S amplifies perceptions and memories beyond what our neurosensory implants can process. That leads to vivid, lifelike hallucinations."

"So, a neuridiot takes your drug, and nothing happens until they turn it on," Cal noted. "How do they do that?"

"With a watch," I said. I held up my wrist to show Klecko and Cal my watch's face. It looked like an analog clock but with one extra hand. "Do you see that thin gold line at one o'clock? That's a low 6S setting. The more I move it clockwise toward twelve, the higher I get, the freakier the hallucinations. I can also turn it backwards to mellow out. Twelve, going counterclockwise, is zero. When I get there, 6S stops working completely."

Cal nodded. Even the pockmarks on his face seemed to smile. "I don't think there's anything like that on the street. Klecko?"

"Interesting. A billion-dollar invention if the high is any good."

"Oh, it's good," I said. "It's better than good. It's a goofy, giggly, better-than-good good. When you turn the control to five o'clock, the highest I tested, the world becomes a carnival fun house."

"How do you get the drug into a neuridiot?" Klecko asked.

"That's open to discussion," I said. "If we do this deal, I'll work with you on the manufacturing process. You can design it to be snorted, misted, taken as a pill—doesn't matter. Once the drug is in a neurosurfer's system, it stays."

Cal took his hands off his beer and tapped his crooked fingers on the tabletop in contemplation. "'Five years in the system,' you said. How much do you think we can sell it for?"

Yes! He said *we*. They were interested.

I smiled. "I don't want to sell 6S. I think we can make more money if we give it away and then charge customers two hundred dollars an hour to access the app."

Cal may have been sly as a billionaire fox, but there would be no poker-facing that price. His eyes popped open, as did Klecko's beady snake eyes. They looked at each other and back at me. "That's a lot of money."

"It's a lot of high."

Klecko tilted his head skeptically. Cal nodded curiously.

"How do they pay you?" Cal asked.

"Through the payment portal on their watch."

I put my hand on the table so they could see the watch's payment band. "Once their payment clears, the gold line shows at twelve o'clock. They can turn it up and down for as long as they pay."

"How do you get your app through the paywalls? The watchmakers will report you to the feds as soon as you apply."

"My app has a hack to bypass their trolls and tolls." I paid myself two hundred dollars to show them how it worked.

Klecko and Cal glanced at each other, then looked back at me. Cal's finger tapping stopped. He turned the poker face back on. He still did the talking, his voice calm and measured. "Two hundred dollars for an hour. What if they buy a few minutes and take the watch off?"

"They won't," I said. "The hallucinations are too intense. Anyone who uses 6S is going to want to dial it back every few minutes, if only to see what's real and what's not."

Cal nodded, though he kept his poker face. "You give neuridiots the drug. Then they have to pay you to control it."

"That's right." I beamed.

"Smart," said Cal. "Where do we fit in?"

I set my drink aside and rested my hands on the table. My best Devita Duran business-talking posture. "You guys have two things I don't: a lab to manufacture drugs at scale and a network to get them out on the street."

"The opps we built to push Duplextacy," noted Klecko.

"Exactly. The business I gave you. Here's what I'm giving you now. You guys manufacture the 6S and use your network to get it on the street with the app. Then, anytime someone pays me to get high, you get twenty-five percent."

Klecko and Cal looked at each other. "Wow, twenty-five percent," said Klecko, stretching out each syllable as he looked back at me.

"Good deal, isn't it?"

Cal frowned. This would not be an easy negotiation. "Let me get this straight," he said. "We use our lab to make your drug. Do we supply the raw materials, too?"

I firmed up my expression. I could be a tough negotiator, too. "Yes, it's your equipment. You know what chemical specs work best. Whatever you choose, the raw materials are cheap. And you'll be getting twenty-five percent of sales. Right off the top."

Cal nodded. "Our materials. Our labs. Our people. We put up the money, we rejigger our labs and operations, we buy all the supplies, we put our network on the line to distribute your free drug. And when the money comes in, we get a whopping twenty-five percent of the take."

The *whopping* was clearly sarcastic. Maybe my offer wasn't as good as I thought. "I can go to thirty percent," I said.

They said nothing. Cal's slicked-back hair turned an angry, foxy orange. Klecko's snakes tensed up and writhed.

"Thirty-five?" I offered.

Again, Klecko and Cal said nothing. But Cal's ears woke to attention, and the snakes on Klecko's arm stirred. Maybe I was getting somewhere.

"Thirty-eight percent?" I offered.

Cal shook his head and laughed, dropping all pretenses of a poker face. Klecko's half smile slanted toward his ear. I'd seen this look whenever he'd left the lab to collect a debt.

"Forty, and I'll split the cost of supplies with you," I said. I could play hardball, too. "That's my final offer."

"I have a counter proposal," said Cal.

Klecko's snake-skinned arm dropped onto my wrist-watched hand and held it. Really held it. And not in a giggly, smoochy, we're-about-to-get-all-kissy kind of way.

Cal lifted a hand from his beer and dropped two fingers into his breast pocket. "Let's say Klecko and I broke into that, ha-ha, lab of yours on the way to this meeting and found this little sample of—what is it called? 6S?"

Oh My Tables TurnedNess! Cal pulled out a vial. It belonged to me. And so did the frenetic swirl of shape-shifting gels and gasses inside it. He twirled the vial within his three crooked fingers as nimbly as a majorette twirls a baton, a move he had to have practiced.

"What can you do with it?" I said. "There are only five doses in there."

"Our lab's more sophisticated than when you worked for us," Cal said. "We can reverse engineer this."

I held back a laugh. "I doubt that. Don't you see the living chemical reactions in that vial? There are more misdirects in the formula than mirrors in a fun house." This was no bluff. Klecko and Cal needed me if they wanted to make sense of 6S or any other high-value psychoactive they pinched from my lab.

"We'll see about that," said Cal.

"It doesn't work like any drug you know how to make," I said. "And it's worthless without my software."

I tried to pull my hand away. Klecko tightened his hold and twisted my hand with the grip he used for bill collections. If I moved a millimeter, bones would fracture. If I tried to get away, bones would shatter.

"We can reverse engineer that, too," said Cal. His foxlike eyes pierced into mine with the intense concentration of a wild animal cornering its prey. Klecko stared, too. The snakes on his arm came alive.

"No, you can't." My voice cracked. I must have sounded like a

B-grade green screener in a bogus death scene.

But I wasn't acting or lying. No existing decompiler could crack 6S or the software on my watch. 6S didn't work like other drugs. They needed me. Yet Cal grinned. And Klecko grinned more.

Oh My ExpendableNess! Klecko and Cal didn't know how complex and uncrackable these formulas were. Which, in their mind, made me gulpingly disposable.

So, I gulped.

Maintaining that bone-shattering grip, Klecko lifted my hand off the table. "She told us she never tested 6S past the five o'clock setting." He spoke to Cal but looked at me.

"Probably couldn't handle more than that," Cal replied. His ears grew pointier, meaner, and more foxlike.

Klecko used his free hand to poke my face. He made me look at his now snake-like face and into his all-green eyes. "Right now, the little gold hand's at one, so you're hardly hallucinating, right?" he said.

I said nothing. This meeting was going to be the death of me, and not in a figurative, gee-I'm-frustrated kind of way.

"RIGHT?" Klecko repeated. He tightened his bone-shattering grip.

I swallowed. "Right."

Klecko put his meaty index finger on the gold pointer. His soft touch matched my pressure settings. I'd forgotten how smooth he could be. "If I turn this forward to twelve, you hallucinate to the max, right?"

"Right," I said, choking on a swallowed whisper.

"And if I take this watch away, you can't dial 6S back. You'll have no way to know what's real and what's not, right?"

I nodded, if only to spare myself a shattered hand.

"And it's going to stay in your system for five years."

Oh My Cement OvershoesNess! Was this how they planned to off me?

Klecko chuckled. With a smooth, calibrated touch, he turned the thin gold dial forward until it maxed out at 12:00. "Have fun," he said.

He ripped the watch off my wrist and slid out of the booth with Cal.

I guessed they left the bar but couldn't be sure. My reality shattered like stained glass in a batting cage.

PENELOPE

Sixty years ago, scientists sought to counter depression, PTSD, and other mental health maladies with microelectronic brain implants. Half the subjects in the study committed suicide. The other half went on murderous rampages.

It was the first clinical trial in history where deaths outnumbered subjects.

"We can fix this glitch," insisted the device's advocates in congress. (They were also the manufacturer's biggest stockholders.) Two years later, scientists tested neurosensory implants.

These chips muffled and reprocessed sensations of sight, sound, smell, taste, and touch, along with memories. The user's diminished experience reduced the intensity of the chemical reactions in their brain. Subjects became calmer and more pliable.

To a government for the people by the people, a mellower, more pliant population puts less stress on health and social service systems. By law, everyone gets implants during infancy. Scientists say colors are duller and sounds are softer than what people experienced in the last century. We all grow up with constant interruptions of pleasure and pain.

If today's bars rollick like hyenas on nitrous, yesterday's ruckused like monkeys on cocaine.

Yet, the technology also leaves people with an unyielding desire for richer, more sensual experiences. Bars and dope lounges do a brisk business. Sex toys are more inventive and ubiquitous. Legal stimulants from caffeine and nicotine to Ritalin and Adderall support a huge portion of the economy. A lot of people are getting rich off neurosensory implants.

But nobody's getting richer than underground psycho-pharmacists. The market for illegal mood and sensation enhancers is so big, police departments can't enforce the anti-drug laws. There's no shortage of chemicals to alter your brain chemistry.

And no maker of psycho-pharmaceuticals has ever topped Devita Duran creations. I sub-majored in biobotics, organic robots. While some entrepreneurs used this science to create smart sex toys, I hacked implants.

I designed 6S to hijack the implants, tricking them out to amplify senses, not muffle them. Shocked by overload, the technology sought context in conscious and unconscious memories, also exaggerated by 6S. Lacking the bandwidth to handle this overload, the overworked implants layered hallucinations over the user's experience.

My 6S app let users control the sensory amplification, and with that, their hallucination's intensity and freakiness. Still, no app could prepare you—or me—for the sudden 6S jump from the 1:00, near minimum, to 12:00, the max.

Donlon's burst into a frenzy of ROY G. BIVs. The music and chatter exploded into a cacophony of bangs, clangs, pops, and buzzes. Taste, smell, and touch raucoused into pandemonium. Senses splintered and splintered and splintered into ever more granular pixels. Everything swirled into a dark, silent absence of sensation.

I don't know how long I was out before the spinning senses came back together. Touch returned first; my clothes felt chocolaty, and the seat beneath me seemed minty. Nothing was as it should have been. The bar sounded green and blue. The people looked loud and discordant.

Eventually, the whirlwind slowed—my brain's neurosensory implant coming to terms with the elevated level of 6S. When the spinning stopped, I no longer sat at a table in a tavern but by a tree stump in the woods. A smooth, brightly colored tree stump with exaggerated delineations in its rings and knots. The benches were gone.

My butt rested on a mound of mud. Its softness defied reality.

Everything around me defied reality.

Oh My Yaba Daba DooNess! Donlon's was now a cartoon riverbank. And not a modern, all-but-real cartoon. I was in a flat, mid-twentieth-century animation, the kind I'd learned about in college film classes.

The blue-green river that flowed in place of the bar produced the same ripples after ripples, time after time. Along the riverbank, animated rats, cats, dogs, wolves, rabbits, and asses sported ugly, expensive suits. The animals made all kinds of sounds—they squealed, yapped, and chirped at each other—but only cat feces flowed from their mouths.

A gag-worthy cheese odor emanated from the back of the bar. There, where the jukebox had been, three chipmunks sang about a witch doctor.

Oh My Ooh Eeh Ooh Ah AhNess! This wasn't a new high. This was a new world.

A Yogi Bear lookalike stood in the middle of the river. He pulled an iridescent salmon from the water and tossed it up the river to a psychedelic peacock. The peacock turned into a listless wolf, head down and tail to the ground.

A tweet from a little titmouse sent Yogi diving into the water. He came up with several trout and tossed them to the little boobless bird. She flew alongside the tree stumps, dropping fish along the way.

A wiggling, shimmering fish landed in front of me.

No way I ordered that. I don't drink fish. Did someone buy it for me? Bick Johnstone? Creepo Manchuo? I looked up and down the riverbank. Nobody—actually, no animal—looked back.

I found the buyer by the dark mouth of a cave, where Donlon's door had been. A panting dog, a three-dimensional CGI creation, stood out against the flat cartoon backdrop. He looked like a German Shepherd but bigger and redder. A long tongue lapped from his mouth in a relentless pant.

I had an admirer.

More of an admirer than I wanted. He turned his head, but his eyes remained locked on me, sliding to the side and back of his head as he buried his face between his hind legs. He put his tongue to work, staring at me while he got his mojo up.

A vibration inside my left thigh interrupted my gag reflex. I reached into the hidden telephone pocket, now a biological sac, and pulled out a lobster. Not a cartoon lobster, a real one. Well, more real than my—wait, did I now have a hoof?

Oh My Animal MagnetismNess. I didn't have a phone in my hand. I had a lobster stuck to the pads of a hoof. Did that mean...?

I turned my head toward the river. Sure enough, the reflection showed a droopy, wide-eyed face looking back.

A cow. A cartoon cow. I knew I had boobs, but a cow?

The crustacean's claws clattered like a speed freak's castanets. With my second hoof, I pushed its stomach. The clattering stopped. The lobster's stalked black eyes retreated into a face of brown and gray fur. Actually, not fur, but sharp, needly quills. The mandibles turned into whiskers around a twitching mouth. An elongated pink nose grew, surrounded by the lobster's antennae.

"Penelope!" I called.

Penelope Coyne was my best friend and assistant. I didn't know why 6S had turned her into a rat-nosed porcupine, except that she was no Devita Duran in the looks department.

"What happened to you?" Penelope said. "You look like someone conked a cow on the head."

"You're not looking so great, either," I said.

I told her about my meeting with Klecko and Cal. How they'd rejected my offer, stolen my watch, and left me among the animals in an old cartoon. Somehow, despite the hoof hands, lobster phone, and quilled face in front of me, my voice and sanity remained oddly intact.

"Wow," she said.

Wow was right. Nothing was more hideous than bulging spikes around the eyes of a shocked porcupine. Especially when twitching green antennae stretched apart the pink nostrils of its ratty nose.

Penelope sure was ugly.

"You need to get your watch back," Penelope said.

"No, I need to get to my lab and formulate an antidote."

Two mules glared at me on their way to the cave and out of the forest.

The chipmunk music ended, and the cheesy odor got worse, devolving deeper into nursing-home pop. Or, as my 6S mind heard it, a tropical bird squawking about Monica, Erica, Rita, Tina....

I lowered my voice. I didn't need corp. dorks in my life, or by my side, or hearing what I saw.

"You can't go to your lab," Penelope said. "That's why I called. Look at the security videos."

"How? The bar's a river, and the patrons are forest animals. What's my lab going to be? A mystery mash buffet?"

The rat-nosed porcupine closed its eyes. After a moment of contemplation, Penelope said, "Okay, I'll tell you what you can't see. Your lab's ransacked. Someone broke in, knocked over the cabinets, smashed every bottle, and tore all the containers open. Your mini fridge is on its side, with the door ripped off and its guts spilled out. The floor's a carpet of eye-spinning psychedelics."

Not good. I needed those chemicals.

"Is there anything to work with?" I asked Penelope.

"No," she said. "Whoever did this set the Henson burner to spray and randomized your decompilers' and recompilers' commands. They're zapping all your supplies and equipment into aberrant states of matter. Your lab's a room full of unknown chemicals and gasses."

"I can figure something out."

"Devita, you're maxed out on 6S. If you walk in there, you won't know what you're seeing, smelling, or touching. You need your watch."

"I don't have my watch."

"You need to find Klecko and Cal and take it back from them."

"Find Klecko and Cal? In a city the size of New York? I'd have a better chance of finding the Thursday Night Strangler."

"It's only Wednesday."

"That's my point. My chance of finding them is zero."

"Devita, use the tracker on your phone."

I turned the lobster left, right, over, and upside down. "What tracker? Right now, I'm talking to a porcupine-faced lobster." No need to mention the rat nose. Penelope knew she was ugly.

"If your phone has a tracker, your lobster has one, too,"

Penelope said. "You call the drug 6S because it's short for sixth sense, as in Extra Sensory Perception. Everything you see, hear, touch, smell, and taste is reality amplified."

"Amplified? I'm sitting at a tree stump near a river, watching a bear toss fish to foxes, rabbits, wolves, and a titless bird."

Penelope's shock gave way to a face full of smiling spikes. The antennae twisted to the sides of the nostrils and curled up to form their own smile. Did I have to look at her?

"Devita, don't be so nervous," Penelope said. "You've already figured this out. Donlon's is a watering hole, and that big guy behind the bar always reminded you of a cartoon bear. Look at all the sly, vicious, and horny characters saying nothing worthwhile. It's happy hour on a work night. All you're seeing is a 6S amplification of reality."

I nodded. "Okay, but how does a lobster amplify my phone?"

"Hard case. Antennae. Built-in navigation system. All things you need right now."

"Right. And the navigation can take me to my apartment."

"What's there?"

"Food. Bed. Couch. Or whatever they look and feel like to me now. I can hang there until I get new chemicals to synthesize an antidote. Or a new watch to program."

Penelope shook her porcupine face. "You don't have time, Devita. You're too out of it to write software the feds won't catch. And even if you get chemicals and machinery for your lab, you won't know what they are."

"That's crazy. I've been working with these chemicals since high school."

"Not while maxed out on 6S. You can't work in a lab until you decode your hallucinations. Otherwise, you'll pick up a glass of cat piss thinking it's orange juice when it's really trimethoxyphenethylamine."

Penelope had a point. Even under the least hallucinated of circumstance, it's never a good idea to mix psychedelics while eating and drinking. But home was still the safest option. "How long will it take to decode these visions" I asked. "A week?"

"Maybe more. By the time you figure out what's what, Klecko and Cal can crack your formulas and software. They've got zillions in

Duplextacy profits to work with. You don't know how sophisticated their lab might be."

"Who cares? Once I have an antidote for 6S or a new watch, I'll out-formulate them and trump whatever product they made from mine."

Penelope's antennae jumped and twirled in a panic. Her rat nose trembled like a ladybug on a hedge trimmer. "If you try that, they'll kill you. These are bad people, remember?"

"Why didn't they kill me now?"

Again, Penelope closed her eyes, demonstrating that a ponderous porcupine was more revolting than a shocked one.

"They know you added misdirects to the formula. They think that after a few schizophrenic days, you'll work for them. But if they crack the 6S first, they won't need you. They won't want your competition. They'll kill you. Getting your watch back is the only way to save yourself and stop them."

"But getting my watch back means finding them. And when I find them, what am I supposed to do? They have guns. I have hallucinations."

"Your hallucinations are your edge. Remember what I told you? You call the drug 6S because the underlying hypersensitivity that drives your illusions amount to a sixth sense. At twelve o'clock, you're practically a prophet."

"A prophet? If that big dog licking his built-in lollipop is a prophecy, I'd rather be an atheist."

I must have said that too loud. A pair of rabbits, eyeing my tree stump from the riverbank, moved to the back of the bar.

"Ignore that dog," Penelope said. "We're going to find the lab, burst in guns blazing, and grab your watch."

"What guns? I don't carry."

"No, but Cheech and Troy do. You wouldn't use them if they didn't."

"They're freelance bouncers, not gunslingers."

"That's what you think. Cheech and Troy love a good gunfight. Especially when you're paying them time and a half."

"Paying them what?" I must have shouted that. The animals in the forest stopped barking, cawing, and whatever they were doing. The dog, too, released his lollipop to pant in my direction. Only the fading voice of the polyamorous bird remained.

"Now's no time to bargain," said Penelope.

The music got softer and slower, a bullfrog crying because someone left his cake out in the rain. I brought my voice down. "I'm paying two high-priced bouncers time and a half—"

"And me," Penelope interrupted. All those smiling spikes and antennae grew. "I'm the closest thing you have to a level-headed guide right now."

"I'm paying three people time and half to go on a wild goose chase. By the time I get to the lab, I'll be broke. And dead."

"It's not a wild goose chase," Penelope said. "You can follow your watch on your phone. I mean lobster."

"How do I follow my watch with a lobster," I cried. Oops, I said that too loud—again. More heads turned my way, including my not-so-secret admirer. He flapped his tongue in my direction. He drooled from every orifice in his head and body. *Every* orifice.

"Let me have your lobster," Penelope said.

"Why, are you hungry?"

"No, let me have the controls. Twist the lobster's tail to my face."

I turned the tail up. Penelope's porcupine mouth bit it. The lobster shed its shell, revealing a body of white meat crosshatched with pink veins. The same shade as Penelope's twitching nose. Not like any lobster I'd ever eaten, but cool. "Is that a map?"

"Yes, and that blue blood clot moving through the pink primary artery is your watch. Do you see where it's headed?"

"Yes, but I'm hallucinating. How do you know what I'm seeing?"

Penelope shook her head. "We don't have time for that now. Do you see where the hematoma's headed?

"I can't tell."

"It's going downtown," Penelope said. "When you leave the forest, walk in the same direction as your lobster's blood clot."

"I won't know where I'm going or what I'm seeing."

"Yes, you will. Look around. You've never had a clearer vision of who's a proud peacock, a sly fox, a cuddly bear, a hungry wolf…"

"A horny dog."

Penelope shook her head. Her spiked furs vibrated like nervous guitar strings. "Go into that cave," she said. "You're Devita Duran. You can do it. Once you're out on the street, you can decode the visions and follow your lobster to your watch. When the clot stops moving, you'll know they're at their lab."

"Then what?"

"Cheech and Troy and I will also be following it. If you leave now, you'll be close behind. You'll catch up with us at the lab. Then we'll go in together and take back your watch."

The porcupine face disappeared and left me looking into the lobster's horror-movie eyes. It had no shell. In the meat, a blue blob moved through a pink grid.

I left the booth. The bullfrog in the back of the bar left. A cat took his place. She mewed about life as a cow bitch:

"Moo, I'm a cow bitch."

I could relate. My reflection in river left no doubt about my present existence. Moo. I was a cow right down to the cleft in my hooves. But I could also be a bitch.

I clasped the trout in my hoof's cleft and left the booth.

My canine admirer set aside his personal entertainment center to pant at me. I threw the trout at him and stepped into the mouth of the cave.

Wait! What just happened? I hallucinated—no, envisioned—throwing a fish at a dog. But did I just throw a drink at some guy?

And what about Penelope? I'd told her my phone was a lobster, but, "Twist the lobster's tail into my face." "That blue blood clot moving through the main artery is your watch." "Go into the cave." I'd never told Penelope that Donlon's entrance became a cave. How could she know what I saw and did?

Had she gotten into my brain or…?

Oh My Straight JacketNess! Did 6S turn everything Penelope and I said to each other into a hallucinated alternate reality?

If so, what had I said to her?

31

What had she said to me?

There was no time to worry about that. Penelope and I could suss all that out when I got my watch and non-schizophrenic brain back. But until then, I couldn't rely on anything I saw, said, or heard.

Not good. But I had no choice. I had to get to my watch. I stumbled into the cave, and my reality shattered again.

MOOO

6S, I soon realized, had presented Donlon's door as a cave opening because it led to another world. But my implants had to adjust. Before I could process my first glimpse of the street, my senses again broke apart and swirled into pixelated darkness. But only for a second. Coming out of the whirl, traffic sounded red, the nighttime street looked salty and sour, and everything smelled like a high-pitched tuning fork.

A sharp peck on my shoulder shocked me out of the spin and into my warped reality. I must have been blocking Donlon's door. I stepped to the side and tripped. It could have been a goodbye-kneecap moment, but I landed on a soft, bulbous mass. It released a delighted squeal.

My eyes—or whatever I saw with—recovered a semblance of vision. A purple-eyed pig had cushioned my fall. Not a cartoon pig but not quite real, either. Too pink. It rubbed its face against sharp crags that jutted from the muddy ground. A gag-worthy blend of piss, poop, puke, and bubble gum emanated from its rear as it squealed in pleasure.

Decode your visions, Penelope had said. That pig had to be one of those masochistic bums, a newly common blight on the streets of New York. I rolled off it into a dirt path. Two giant creatures, an armadillo and a hamster, sniffed at my armpits. Good Samaritans, for sure. I let them help me to my....

Hooves. Like every creature on the street, I had no hands or feet.

We all had hooves, claws, paws, fins, or flippers. Except those that had the toes, talons, or webbed feet of birds.

"Thank you," I said to the armadillo and hamster.

They ran away from me.

I scouted my surroundings and—Oh My Creepy ClownNess!—6S and the night's darkness had conspired to conjure New York's ongoing demise as a dead carnival. Boarded-up sideshows, ticket booths, rides, and games lined the dirt path that earlier tonight had been the craggy, uneven sidewalk and potholed blacktop of a Midtown side street.

This was no cartoon. It looked real. Or, at least, as real as a cheap fan-made *Blade Runner* remake. 1970s FX and all. In it, the once greatest city in the world looked deader than Creepo Manchuo's chance of scoring with that blond. Or anyone.

The shuttered rides—6S creations for sure—saddened me the way any dilapidated amusement park might have. But the 6S-generated memories and details seemed off. I mourned mazes without rats. Maggot tamers without meat to thrill their audiences. Centipedes stuck in glue traps, unable to give children rides.

Only the fun houses, with their mirrored facades, lived. Animals stumbled out of the reflections. A steady flow of creatures—everything from anteaters to zebras—went up, down, and across the paths. Those that came in my direction warped around a frozen, dazed-out me.

What had Penelope said about decoding proud peacocks and sly foxes? And where were they? The five- and six-foot gerbils and aardvarks I saw possessed no human qualities. Those slobbering monkeys might have been sloppy drunks. Or just monkeys. In front of me, the carrier pigeon might have been an air taxi. But two rabbits, paw-in-paw, jumping on board? How was I supposed to make sense of that vision?

So many animals plodded down this path, and the more I tried to figure out what they were, the weaker my hold on reality became.

My lobster, attached to my hoof, was useless. The blue blood clot snailed through its pink veins, slow enough that a normal me could have caught up to it. But nothing was normal. I didn't know where it was, where I was, or how to move.

I stood on the sidewalk watching these passing animals avoid me by wider and wider margins. The neurosensory implants filled my ears and addled my brain with random grunts, howls, hoots, hollers, chirps, clucks, coos, hisses, and squeaks. My skin quivered hot and cold and wet and dry. Never mind the smells.

A despondent, horny-looking wolf stumbled out of the mirror where Donlon's had been. Apart from his pack, he slouched, head down, like the alpha dog had gotten the better of him. Again.

Finally, a vision I could understand. The guy was a real-life loser. One of those beta dogs that couldn't win at work or play.

Candidly, I had a thing for beta dogs. The grosser ones I blew off. Creepo Manchuo wasn't the first guy who got a "serve booze at your wake" response to the offer of a drink.

Sometimes I fantasized about going home with beta dogs. I wanted to give these losers the best body they could never hope to touch, a night that would make a ten-thousand-dollar hooker blush. Then, come morning, I would say, "You're the kind of guy that makes women lesbians." Or ask, "Did you use those sandpaper hands to grind down your equipment?" My favorite fantasy: get out of the apartment before the guy woke up and leave him a note. "Had to leave early. Saw your morning face and almost threw up."

I liked to mess with guys' heads.

But this beta dog had a weird effect on me. Seeing him made me want to mate. I mean, really mate. But I had no time to pursue him. A clattering on my hoof had to take priority. My lobster was ringing.

I raised my foreleg. My lobster had stuck to one half of the cleft in my hoof. The other half of the cleft moved to the belly and pressed it. Two quill-framed eyes looked back at me. "Devita," Penelope scolded. "Why are you still at Donlon's?" The antennae sticking out of her nose shook admonishingly.

"Donlon's? Is that where I am? I thought I left. I thought I was on the street."

"You are. On the sidewalk outside Donlon's door. You haven't moved in ten minutes. What are you doing?"

"Watching animals avoid me by wider and wider arcs."

"You've got to get moving," Penelope cried. "Look at your

phone."

"I don't have a phone. I have a lobster on the verge of an embolism."

"Look at the belly."

"Why do I see two creepy coagulums now?"

"One of them is black, right? The size of a pen dot?"

"How do you know that?"

Penelope apparently took that answer as a *yes*. "That's me, Cheech, and Troy," she said. "We're on Klecko and Cal's trail. Why aren't you moving?"

"Because I don't know where I am or where to go."

Once again, 6S treated me to the gruesome face of a concerned porcupine. The pink rat nose bulbed out a bit. The antennae rattled. "Devita, trust your visions. They're exaggerations of reality."

"Easy for you to say. I'm in a dead circus surrounded by oversized animals and fun-house mirrors. I don't know what reality they're exaggerating."

"Oh, you poor girl. You need your watch."

"You keep telling me that. But I don't have a matchstick's chance in a nuke of finding it."

Penelope showed me another moment of hideous contemplation. "I have another idea," she said. "Don't decode the hallucinations. Lean into them. Accept your existence as a cow, or whatever else 6S turns you into, and move forward through the world as you see it."

"Move forward? From where? I don't know where I am."

"Devita, you don't need to know where you are to go to where you're going. Trust your lobster. If the black and blue blobs get bigger, you're going in the right direction. If they get smaller, it's the wrong way. Let your hematomas take you to Cheech, Troy, and me. Then we'll get your watch back and you can turn off the 6S."

I nodded. Penelope ended the call.

I had to move. The creepy crawlers in my lobster's artery were getting away from me. Last I remembered, I was closer to Seventh Avenue, a downtown street. Penelope had said Klecko and Cal were going downtown. But as I took a few steps toward Seventh Avenue, my lobsters' pink veins squeezed the blue blob smaller.

I turned to go the other way, and things got strange.

The raging river that was Eighth Avenue flowed uptown. Still, the blue blob grew as I went toward it. Klecko and Cal were going downtown on an uptown street. They could be taking an air taxi. But if they were, their blood clot would be moving faster.

The downtown subway on Eighth Avenue could also explain my lobster's behavior. But why would Klecko and Cal take the subway? If I were them, I'd want to get to the lab as soon as possible.

There had to be a logical explanation. But I was too impaired to consider the possibilities.

Penelope was right. My hallucinations were my reality. I had to go where my lobster's bloodstream took me.

I joined a growing crowd of oversized hamsters, gerbils, possums, anteaters, and aardvarks that headed toward the raging river that might have been Eighth Avenue. As I neared the riverbank, I passed a fun house and looked into its warped mirror.

Where was that face Helen of Troy would envy? Were those big round eyes, black nose, and furry cheeks mine? Were those wide hind quarters my hips? And what about the swollen udder ballooning over my chest? The hanging, overextended teats?

Oh My Life's so StrangeNess! In two hours, I went from *Meme Girl of the Century* to Dairy Farm Calendar Model.

Mesmerized by the mirror, I watched the scrawny armadillo behind me morph into another cow. As did all of the animals on this march to the river—lions, rats, tigers, horses, and lonely wolves; I turned away from the mirror and watched as 6S turned them all into cows.

What did this mean? Had everybody in New York grown boobs like mine?

If Penelope was right, I had to stop interpreting these visions and live in the moment. Or moo-ment, considering my current circumstances.

Me and my fellow cows marched with the singular purpose of a meaty herd. I dropped my head like a proper bovine. My lobster, clinging low on my foreleg near my right hoof, twisted to show me the blue and black blobs in the pink vein. The blue clot bulged out. I was going in the right direction. The herd was leading me to my watch.

Or, so I thought.

Where the path ended near the river's edge, I joined the other cows, squeezing through a fenced-in path that led us down a steep hill. At the bottom, the herd fanned out, separating into single-file lines in which cows headed one-by-one toward narrow chutes, also fenced in.

One of my college boyfriends had turned me on to slaughterhouse videos, so I knew what this was. But I'd never seen this from the cow's point of view. At the end of this chute, a large metal pistol would shoot a bolt through my skull.

I backed up away from the herd and into a wet snout.

I looked over my shoulder. A large pit bull mounted my hindquarters and rubbed his bullishness against my rump. Panting. Drooling. Humping.

Was this love in the time of 6S?

Cow bitch meets pit bull?

Was 6S trying to show me that some guy liked me? If so, he liked me a lot. The pit bull wrapped his forelegs around my ribcage and pawed at my thick, heavy teats.

No, this wasn't love. This was a pervert jumping a cow, not caring that she wasn't in heat.

I wanted to yell at him, but nothing came out of my mouth except "Moo, moo." His paws pressed into my teats. His right paw moved to my udder's side and dug its claws into my rib cage. I tried to shake him off. His claw dug further in. Definitely a perv.

Maybe in old America, someone in this crowd would have come to my rescue. But in today's mind-your-own-business Amerika, where neurosensory implants modulate mood-altering perceptions, nothing would happen. Perceptions of my predicament landed too far into the periphery to incite anger or action.

Fortunately, my business brought me toe-to-toe (and other body parts to other body parts) with all kinds of crude, horny guys. I knew when to play nice and when to get mean. And when none of that worked, how to shock my nemesis with advanced street-fighting moves nobody would expect from a hottie like me.

But in the here and now, I wasn't a hot babe. And I wasn't up against a guy. This battle pitted a bull-sized pit bull against his happy humping ground. Namely me.

The clinging claw broke from my rib cage, and his paw moved back to my teats. Perfect. I could make my move without his claws ripping my hide. I brought my haunches down, then up. The pit bull went up and over my bovine shoulder and landed with a thud on his back.

A paw dug into one of my forelegs. With my other foreleg, I stomped and stomped and stomped on his mouth, shredding his lips and chin. His face looked like bean curd noodles in too much tomato sauce.

And he was mad.

The pit bull jumped to his hind legs, growling and baring his canines. The pointy teeth turned into glistening, metal fangs. Daggers burst from his front paws. White, rabid foam frothed from his mangled mouth.

Caught between a ferocious cur and a slaughterhouse bolt pistol, I was done. And not in a yay, project over, pat-on-the-back kind of way.

But wait! If that deranged pit bull could stand on two legs, so could a bovine Devita Duran. And Devita Duran had something no rabid cur could claim: ballet lessons as a six-year-old.

I jumped to my hind legs and brought my forelegs over my head, interlocking the two halves of my hooves. So positioned, I twirled, sliding forward, bouncing from one side of beef to the next. And the next. And the next.

I tried to dance my way to the side and away from the herd, but the forward momentum was too strong. Behind me, the pit bull growled. I had to go forth into the chute.

I came to a hooded slaughterer, his face shrouded in shadows. The pistol loomed larger than any I had ever seen. A blunt metal cylinder extended from the handle toward my forehead.

Fortunately, a dancing cow in fifth position en haut has options. Before the slaughterer could land the bolt gun between my eyes, I dropped a hoof onto his head.

On one hand, or hoof, the move worked. I got through the chute alive. I also escaped the pit bull. Glancing back, I saw him retreat from the chute.

But to get to this point without a hot metal slug in the forehead, I'd had to conk the slaughterer with my lobster. Had I damaged my navigation system? Killed it?

Hard to tell. Passing through the chute, I experienced a brief shattering of reality. A very brief shattering. In the time it took to catch my breath, reality splintered then swirled into pixelated darkness.

My senses reassembled in a brooding, black-and-white underworld, a tunnel as gray and moody as an art-house exercise in existential nihilism.

Was my lobster still attached to my foreleg? No, it hung from the empty arm of a robe. I had no hands, no feet, no body, and no head. My incorporeal existence wore a flowing, black-cowled robe that descended to where my feet should have been.

DEAD AND DEADER

Was I dead? Was everyone around me dead? No longer one cow in a herd, I was now one of many faceless souls descending into a shadowed goth stadium. Around me, more grim reapers strode leglessly to the underworld to a single-note dirge.

My lobster squirmed and stuck out its belly. On it, gray and black spots moved forward through lighter gray veins. The navigation system still worked. More importantly, the blood clot pulsed larger.

I didn't know if I was dead or alive, but at least I was going in the right direction.

One spirit, not like others, came toward me. Dressed in a bathrobe with loud-ringing bells on its hood and chest, it radiated trouble.

"Stop!" it shouted.

Oh My What NowNess! This spirit had a face. Another German Shepherd. But this one's eyes remained firmly in the front of its head, and there was no rise between its legs that I could see. Just the annoyed face of a lazy guard dog that would rather be sleeping.

"Where's your coin?" it said.

"What coin?"

"You need a coin to board the River Styx ferry. Without it, you can't descend to the underworld. You must stay here forever."

"Someone stole my watch, and there's no money on my lobster."

"Lobster? Hand it over."

"Why, are you hungry?"

"Give it to me."

"Well, if you insist," I said. I raised my armless arm and rammed a sharp edge of the lobster's shell into the German Shepherd's head. Just like I'd hit the slaughterer.

Wait! What had I done? Whose skull did I conk?

I ran. How did I run without legs and feet? No time to think about that. I had a coagulation to catch.

I raced down, down, down to the underworld. Along the way, I hurdled over the many pink, purple-eyed pigs. Their colors popped against this monochromatic universe. They blocked my path in clusters, flagellating each other with chunks of fallen concrete and steel.

I came to the edge of the River Styx. A ferry waited at the riverbank. I tagged onto the crowd of grim reapers that boarded, jumping onto a rising ramp as it closed.

Safely away from Ms. Bells, left barking from the water's edge, I joined a throng of faceless souls on a journey down the River Styx.

Wait!

Safely? River Styx? The point of no return between life and death? Was this my final journey?

I stumbled off the ramp and tried to steady myself. Not easy in choppy waters, especially without arms, legs, or feet. The black-and-white movie I inhabited grew fuzzy and staticky, like poor TV reception in the 1950s. Apparently, 6S had destroyed one underworld hallucination just to bring me to another.

Lost in the snow of static and the shaking of the boat, I fell and rolled into a vertical, blood-stained pole. I grabbed it with my handless hands and, using all the strength my armless arms could muster, pulled myself to my footless feet.

Strange that I had this pole to myself. So many cowled death marchers had boarded this ferry at the riverbank, yet I was alone at this end of the cabin. The other souls had crammed into the other end even though there was a lot of room here. Why?

This ferry cabin was long and narrow; mirrored balls hung from the ceiling. The balls spun, and the static cleared up, leaving me in slinky undergarments and sweating under an intense spotlight, the lone pole dancer in the ferry's disco lounge.

Flashing lights and a loud, heavy-bass rhythm disrupted this black-and-white, noir-like universe. My lobster, tucked into the front of my panties, looked out with beady, unblinking eyes. Its pincers, unrealistically fast-moving, clackety clacked to the music.

The floor shook, breaking my grip on the pole. I fell backward into a pig I hadn't seen when I'd boarded. It lay across five seats of a bench, chewing on its foreleg. It smiled and released an aroma of perfumed puke.

The more things changed, the more the purple-eyed, pink pigs stayed the same.

The boat rocked again. I bounced off the pig, and some invisible force, tugging at my right bra cup, pulled me back to the pole. Underneath the bra, where the pit bull had clawed my rib, my skin felt prickly.

Some hooded heads from the other side of the cabin looked in my direction. Most looked away. A loud melody landed atop the heavy bass, and lights strobed at me. Now I understood. This wasn't a disco lounge. I was the featured performer in the ferry's adult entertainment car.

To soothe the tug and prickliness on my chest, I rubbed my right breast against the pole. The boat rocked. I lost my hold and fell.

I rolled across the cabin. Along the way, the staticky old television environment returned, and I once again became an incorporeal cowled robe.

Another hooded soul helped me up.

"Are you okay?" it said.

What nerve! "Am I okay? You're a ghost, too, you know!"

The boat lurched. I stumbled, and the armless arms of my robe reached for the only available support: my helpless helper's neckless neck.

The other ghosts shrieked. With every rock of the boat, the ends of my robe's sleeves wrapped tighter around my helper's throat.

Passengers tried to pull us apart, but I was afraid to let go.

The ferry stopped. The loading ramp dropped. I released the missing neck and bolted. Parting the crowd with flagellating sleeves, I reached the riverbank.

There, a crowd of melon-headed robots waited to board. I had never been so happy to see cantaloupes, crenshaws, and honeydews. And, unlike the black-cowled souls on the ferry, these melons had faces.

Real faces. Faces with tin-can mouths, lead-weight eyes, cotton-ball ears, and rubber-chicken beaks.

They weren't dead. Maybe I wasn't dead.

The robots cleared a path, but my compromised balance couldn't thread the needle. I stumbled from melon to melon until a spiked orange kiwano scratched my left arm.

Arms. I had arms. They were metal, but they were arms. And at the ends of my arms, I had hands. Little silvery hands with little silvery fingers.

And one of those hands held its lobster for dear robotic life.

The ferry left the riverbank.

Bleeding, bruised, and who knows how dirty from rolling along the floor, I lumbered up a small, steep hill. The tugging at my chest eased when I reached a cave at the top of the hill, but the underside of my bra still pinched.

Even a robot can't escape the tyranny of lingerie.

As I entered the cave, my reality again shattered and swirled into waves of pixelated darkness. The sensations reassembled into a high-noon desert. A bright, scorching sun bounced off the sandy red earth.

My feet morphed into three-toed talons. My legs became spindly, ribbed stalks. Sleek, blue, aerodynamic wings replaced my arms.

Up ahead stretched a long, narrow canyon. When I stepped into the canyon, the cliffs around it turned a bright, flat brown, and the red sand below my feet hardened. The colors exaggerated and flattened.

Oh My Looney TuneNess! I was once again in a twentieth-century cartoon. Did this mean I was back at Donlon's?

The answer from the lobster's belly was no. Clipped to one of my wings, its blue blob grew. I was closing in on Klecko and Cal. More importantly, the blood clot didn't move. My former bosses had reached their lab, and it wasn't far.

The lobster vibrated. Penelope appeared. She still had a

porcupine face. No matter how much my world changed, Penelope was still ugly. Especially when excited.

"Devita, we're outside of Klecko and Cal's lab. Where are you?" Her rat nose had grown, extending farther out of her face and past her antennae.

"Beep beep," I answered. That was all I could say

"Oh, no. 6S has you bad. Let me see where you are."

She muted her phone and looked away. Cheech's face came on. At least, I thought it was Cheech. He'd taken on the look of a rattlesnake. "Devita, go back to the River Styx," he hissed. "Your watch is in Tribeca, the old walled city, and you can only get there through the underworld."

"Beep beep."

Penelope's face reappeared. "You're very close. One pier away. We're waiting for you." Her nose extended farther. It stuck out from her face like a pencil. "Get here, and we'll break into the lab and take back your watch."

I shook my head. If 6S turned Penelope into a pencil-nosed porcupine and Cheech into a rattlesnake, what would it do to Troy? "Beep beep," I said.

A fox's face replaced the porcupine. His ears were pointedly alert, and his tongue hung out, licking his lips like he was anticipating the arrival of a tender morsel of prey. He shook a crippled paw at me.

Had Troy become Cal? Was Cheech Klecko?

"Are you coming?" the Troy-Cal-fox yipped.

I nodded and disconnected.

Something was wrong. Very wrong. How had Penelope and the gang understood my beeping language? How had they known about the River Styx? Surely, 6S translated our conversations into something my hallucinations could grasp. But 6S was also a sensory enhancer. Why did Penelope's nose grow? Did that have anything to do with Cheech and Troy going all snake and fox on me?

And why did they now want me back on the fabled journey from life to death?

I looked at my lobster. With my free wing, I poked the blue blood clot. Calculated travel times appeared. It looked like I could walk to my watch in fifteen minutes. In my current state, twenty. Okay, twenty-five. Or, if I scraped some DNA off my skin to access cash, I could look for a carrier pigeon—or something else that meant air taxi—and get there in five.

But first, I had to get to the end of this canyon.

Purpled-eyed pigs lay along the cliff bases, banging their heads on outcropped rocks and filling the air with the overbearing stench of masochism. Above their listless, self-torturing bodies, billboards for Explosives, Anvils, Portable Holes, and other ACME products lined the canyon walls.

My legs spun like wheels, forming rapid circles as I sped through the canyon, leaving a cloud of dusty sand in my wake.

Up ahead, a pig, lying along the base of the cliff on the canyon's left, stirred. His long tongue reached his hind legs. Unlike the other pigs I'd seen tonight, this one wanted pleasure, not pain.

He stared at me with eyes that were yellow, not purple. His snout was longer and thinner than any pig I'd seen tonight, and his body, in a soon-to-pounce crouch, was no porker.

Well, maybe he was interested in porking, but he was no pig. At least, not in the literal sense. He was a dog. Actually, a coyote, but still a taxonomical canine. He raised his head to look at me. His tongue moved from his mouth to his chin to his belly, from which it licked a postage stamp between his legs.

I was about to walk past an ACME Glue Board poster when the coyote jumped. I stopped short. The coyote flew past me into the poster. It turned out to be one of those live posters with real pest-catching glue. My attacker hit the poster face first, and he stuck in place. He was now a coyote statue with his snout and chest stuck to the wall. Painful as all that must have been, it didn't stop the coyote's tongue from pushing the envelope.

"Beep beep," I said and continued on my leg-spinning way.

At the canyon's end, I faced a row of cacti. I squeezed between two and arrived at the base of a small hill. After a short climb, the trail turned, and I followed it up another small hill. At the top, I came to another cave.

I stepped into it, and—Oh My DarknessNess! My reality

blackened and melted away like marshmallows in a crematorium.

No shattering senses. Instead, 6S split and stretched my existence like strings of soft taffy. Thinner and farther and thinner and farther I pulled until I became a million strands of nothing.

When those strands of nothingness disappeared and my senses returned, I was still nothing.

Oh My Cosmic CircleNess! Had I died again?

Not that rising from the underworld into a foggy cemetery meant I was dead. But whirling around gravestones in a disembodied state is never a good sign.

This time, I didn't even have the goth gown of a grim reaper. I was just a soul with no hold on reality—except a lobster. (And they say you can't take it with you.)

My spirit, if that was what I was, clung to the lobster and the bulging blue blob in its belly. The cemetery faded into an ethereal passage. I was a fog traveling through more fog until the channel split. A fork in the ether.

Looking to my left, one route led to a bright, white holy city of light. Was that supposed to be Heaven? Midtown Manhattan? The route to my right led to the fire and brimstones of Hell. New York's fallen downtown? That hellscape of exploding gas mains, squatter-filled ruins, and hot dog meat of questionable origin?

By now, I don't have to tell you which way my lobster pulled.

HOT BABE IN HELL

I floated through the channel that led to the world of the damned until the ether coalesced into a physical pathway: a bloody road, lined with glistening, half-shattered towers of jagged black glass and twisted metal. On every large, flat surface, electromagnetic, pallid faces of tortured souls stretched and cried in horror. Their chorus of anguish echoed through the canyons of ruins.

"No, not decaf!"

Legs formed under my soul, leading to the return of my body. This time, I was no cow. No melon-headed robot. No flightless bird. I was Devita Duran in a red bodysuit and blue jeans, all form-fitted to accentuate my many assets. Oddly comforting, despite being in Hell.

Maybe Lucifer liked his girls hot.

The growing blood clot on my lobster's belly led down a midnight-black, artificial, CGI-rendered street of crackled brimstone. After some steps, a flame exploded from a crevice in the sidewalk.

I stepped aside to avoid the fire, right into the path of a rolling, purple-eyed pig. The same kind of unrendered, realistic, purple-eyed pig I'd been seeing all night.

I jumped. The pig rolled under me and stopped over the geyser of flame bursting from the sidewalk. Squeals of pleasure erupted from the pig as chunks of its hide burned away.

Other purple-eyed pigs wanted in. They rolled in from every direction, groaning and grunting, trying to push the burning pig aside

49

and take its place atop the fire pit. Instead, they succeeded only at crushing the first pig, pinning it atop the flame while it slowly turned to ash. The burning pig's screeches of ecstasy grew louder until they stopped. Just stopped. No whimpering or crying. The flames had completely cremated the pig.

Now I was confused.

In what kind of Hell did pigs die while blood clots grew on my lobster?

The flame from the sidewalk petered out, and the purple-eyed porkers stopped fighting over the pile of ashes that had been their fellow. Their frustrated grunts faded away. Moans and groans of tortured souls wafted through the darkness.

I followed my growing coagulum through another stretch of brimstone, nearing my watch. Another explosion, this one louder and brighter, erupted from behind me. The illuminating flares revealed a hellscape of craggy, cavernous mountains and burning flesh. And a long shadow next to my own.

Someone or something was following me.

I broke into a run, but my assailant ran faster. A massive hand landed on my shoulder and threw me to the ground. I rolled over to see an odd-looking Satan standing over me. A very odd-looking Satan. He had big orange eyes. A pig's snout jutted from his horned, angular face.

He dug a hand deep into his pants and whipped out a .44 Magnum pistol. The kind Dirty Harry carried. Its authenticity pierced my CGI manifestation of Hell.

Slowly, the Satan lowered to the ground and straddled my waist.

If this pork-nosed Satan was a mugger in real life, he was no run-of-the-mill mugger. He was brutal and deadly. Had 6S taken me through Hell to show me my end?

The Satan pointed the pistol at my head and grabbed at my lobster with his other hand.

Most people would give up their lobsters for their lives. But tonight, my lobster was my life. I held tight, refusing to give it up.

"That must be some lobster," Satan laughed. "Give it to me."

"Why, are you hungry?" I choked. Not the answer he, nor I,

expected to come out of my mouth. Had 6S given me that answer to confuse him? To throw him off his evil game? Or was I just nervous?

The Satan's orange eyes opened wide. He roared a grinding, guttural, angry rasp and ripped at the lobster.

"It won't do you any good," I pleaded. "There's no money on it."

Satan leaned into my face and put the gun against my head.

I spit in his eyes, now bright and orange.

Satan laughed. A hearty laugh that seemed to weaken his pull on my lobster.

I didn't know why spitting had made him laugh so hard, but if it worked, why question it?

I spit and spit and spit again. He laughed harder and harder and harder.

A smattering of purple flecks disrupted the orange in his eyes. The purple flecks multiplied with each spit. Satan rolled off me in hysterics. I rolled on top of him and again spit in his face. His horns retracted into his head, and long, floppy, porcine ears grew in their place.

Through his hysterically oinky laughter, he said, "You can't hurt me. I take Duplextacy."

Oh My Lucky BreakNess! Duplextacy!

Most people, especially the neurosurfers who used Duplextacy, didn't know that the name combined *duplicity* and *ecstasy*. Duplextacy tricked neurosensory implants into presenting pain as pleasure. Being maxed out on 6S, I didn't know how spitting could be so painful to him. But I was only hallucinating spitting. Whatever I was really doing, it was working.

I spit, spit, spit. He weakened with laughter and joy. I pulled the gun from his hand, rolled out from under him, stood up, and shot the Satan, now a lazy pig, in the kneecap. He was now too happy to care about anything. I shot again.

Dirty Harry's .44 Magnum had six shots. I fired two. I saved the four shots That left me with four for Klecko and Cal's lab.

I left the mugger, now a purple-eyed pig moaning orgasmically, and tucked the gun into my waistband.

Another burst of flame revealed a gang of Satans blocking my path down the street. It was more Satans than I could shoot at. More Satans than I could spit at.

And my mouth was dry.

I bolted to my right between two volcanic walls. Upside-down volcanic walls. Lava flowed up the walls into the sky.

The Satans followed. About halfway up the alley, my lobster clattered. I couldn't answer the call, but a glance at the belly revealed a new green blood clot.

Just what I needed. Another coagulation to follow. It was growing. A good sign?

I came to an insulated drum filled with hot coals. I turned the drum on its side, spilling the contents between me and my pursuers.

That was a mistake. The long-legged devils easily hurdled the coals and were now almost at my tail. And not in a kinky, fun, let's-do-it-doggy-style kind of way. Though doggy style might not have been out of the question.

The alley ended at another wall of gravity-defying lava. A terrace of ashy brimstone jutted from the lava flow. A trapeze hung from its edge. I jumped and caught the crossbar.

I raised my legs and dropped them, pumping back and forth and swinging higher and higher until my extended arm reached the terrace's copper railing. I grabbed the railing with one hand. Then another. In a daring display of derring-do, I pulled myself over the railing onto the terrace's flat craggy surface.

I looked over the edge. The Satanic gang jumped to catch the swinging trapeze. Oh, no you don't! I grabbed the rope and pulled the trapeze onto the terrace.

None of them could jump as high as the terrace. The angry orange and purple glares betrayed their high levels of Duplextacy intoxication. No way they could land a shot at me.

But they could wait me out. Flashing big grins, they stared at me. Even their horns smiled.

My predicament reminded me of an old video where the hero scaled a wall one fire escape at a time. I grabbed the crossbar of another trapeze and swung myself up another flight. And another.

The green blood clot on my lobster expanded with each level.

Stopping to catch my breath, I looked down. One Satan stood on the shoulders of another, attempting to reach the trapeze. He got his hands around the bar, made it to the first landing, and dropped the ropes so his buddies could climb.

They were coming after me.

I Tarzanned my way up the terraces, ignoring the ever-present pinch under my right breast, the tugging now concentrated on my nipple.

Near the top of the wall, I ran out of terraces. Eight Satans were coming after me, but only four bullets remained in my gun. And I was hallucinating. My gun could have been a water pistol.

Still, I had to shoot. I was trapped. It would cost me a bullet, but killing one Satan might scare off the others.

Pulling the gun from my waistband, I noticed a green glow reflected off the barrel. Its source: a green door against the lava wall.

I checked my phone. The belly showed one big green light. The same bright shade as the door. Green. Go. A safe destination?

I returned the gun to my waistband and slipped behind the green door.

Immediately, the soft fibers of my being stretched, stiffened, and punched through a honey-colored glow into a steamy, friction-filled, velvet-black void. Breathy vision enveloped me in a sultry wave of intimate warmth. My body pounded and pulsed and pounded and pulsed, thrusting in and out and in and out until an explosive burst released me.

I came to on the oily, faux-stone linoleum floor of a cramped, low-light chamber. A flowing orange, velvet robe, inches from my face, belonged to a brown-bearded lady who sat on a mustard-yellow throne. On her head sat a gold foil party-hat crown adorned with a riot of red, green, and blue gemstones—all dull, plastic, fake.

"What do you think?" said this odd royal, my hallucination's version of a queen.

"Give me that last part again." The same voice as the queen, but it came from under the throne.

A quick kick to my cheek from the sandaled foot under the robe told me that *last part* was mine to repeat.

"Wiggle the acclimated feathers and fuzzy prune juice into a blue bowl, then shake," I said. I didn't know what that meant. Or how it fit into the conversation we must have been having while 6S had adjusted to the change in scenery.

"Sounds right," said the voice from under the throne. "Eunuch, check it out."

Eunuch turned out to be a tall gym-rat type wearing a baby-blue turban. He wore a sleeveless, sequined, lavender vest, opened to reveal a muscular, don't-mess-with-me frame. His harem pants, though they'd be billowy on another body, clung to his thick thighs and shins. He stood against the maroon wall, cramped next to a plush peach tapestry. He held a phone—not a lobster—and his fingers bounced around the screen.

Every color in this room seemed flatter and campier than the next. The atmosphere had the cheap feel of an old XXX film.

"With some of her own catnip, she can pull in a lot of money," said the queen.

My own what?

"Not worth the risk," replied the lower voice.

The queen spoke with a smooth, calculating demeanor. The voice from under the throne was grittier, more gravelly. It also had horrible breath.

"What risk?" said the queen. "Look at those eyes. That fur. How shapely and pliable she is."

I looked at my body. I was a furry kitten lying on its side.

"She won't stay pliable for long," argued the horrid-breathed voice from below.

I tried to stand, but Eunuch leaned a heavy foot on my ribs, flattening me like a wrung-out towel. A stronger, more persistent tugging at my right breast sharpened the pinch under my ribcage. My lobster, on the floor beneath me, poked into my stomach. I twisted to relieve the pinching, and my gun dug into my waist, held in place by some kind of biological sac.

"You're wrong," said the queen. "Catnip can make her docile, and that plump chest could be good for a lot of tuna."

Oh My Change of CareerNess! I was in a cathouse. And more than heavy petting was on the agenda.

"It won't be long before she tries to claw, scratch, and wriggle free," said the seat-of-the-throne voice. "She's smart. She can outnip her own catnip."

I tried to make sense of the conversation. Where was this cathouse? What catnip were they talking about, and how was it my own?

A nuke's worth of halitosis erupted from under the throne, distracting my thoughts. "We don't know what she's on, who gave it to her, or how long it will last."

Eunuch broke into the conversation. "It's the right formula," he said.

The queen nodded, her brown beard scratching against her velvet robe.

The voice from under the throne asked, "Can we make it ourselves?"

"I just did," Eunuch said. He turned his phone face-up and brought it to the throne.

With a satisfied smile, the queen rose from her throne. "She gave us what we wanted with no argument. Imagine if we addicted her to something that compelled obedience."

An answer came not from under the throne but from the queen's backside. A slit in the back of the queen's orange robe exposed her twin: another bearded lady with a face where the queen's butt should have been and a mouth in place of an anus.

"One drug may counteract the other," the butt face insisted. Understandably, she had the breath of an outhouse.

"We can put her on a leash with a collar. Or tie her up in leather straps. She can be good for a ton of tuna a day."

The butt shook its face no. "This pussy's too dangerous. Too many of our customers travel in her circles. Someone could recognize her and blow up our operation. We have to kill her."

What!!!!

"It's hard to kill a girl," said the queen. "We have to dispose of the body, scrub her DNA, eliminate every trace of her."

The ass had a simple solution. "Call Fu," it said.

At the mention of Fu, my teats jerked, distracting me from the asshole's agonizing breath. The pinch on my right ribcage sharpened.

"Fu doesn't come here anymore," said the queen.

"That's because we're expensive," the ass said. "We can give him this girl for free. He'll take her away, dump the body, and it won't cost us a cent."

The queen nodded her head. Slowly at first, then a little quicker.

I should have expected that. When people talk out of their asses, the head doesn't have a chance.

"No need to call Fu," said Eunuch. After releasing my rib from his foot, he crouched and pulled me by the neck to my hind legs. On the way up, I extended and retracted a set of claws, pulling my lobster into my paw and latching it there.

I was tall for a kitten. Almost as tall as the queen. Eunuch pointed to the spot under my chest that pinched. "Look at this," he said to the queen and her ass.

The ass nodded. "She's on Fu's radar."

I could beat this situation. Street-fighting skills. Ballet lessons. A gun between my legs with enough bullets to take out the queen and her ass, along with Eunuch and this Fu character.

The chamber door swung open, and a rabid Doberman stomped in on his hind legs. Angry. Raving mad. Oozing abrasions on his face and chest. Cuts and scabs marring his chin and lips. Yet, like every canine I'd seen tonight, his dick stood out of its socket. A tongue reached from behind his testicles to lick it. The dog looked horny enough to hump the tapestry. But he glared in my direction.

With a swift slash of my foreleg, I broke the eunuch's grip and pulled the gun from my sac. It felt oddly comfortable in my kitty paws.

The eunuch, the queen, her butthead, and the Doberman backed off. Like a hood in an early twentieth-century flick, I waved the gun to show them where I wanted them: opposite the door with their backs to the wall, next to the throne.

The room was tight. Too tight for four bodies, including one with an extra head on its ass. I squeezed in front of them to get to the door. I opened it and slipped out.

The Doberman jumped. I slammed the door on his snout. I opened it and slammed it again. And again.

The Doberman stepped back from the door. I slammed it shut.

The throne room had a large outer chamber. Very large. The desk alone occupied more floor space than the throne room. And the several chairs behind and near the desk were bigger than the throne.

No time to question that strange architectural priority. I threw a chair in front of the door to slow them down and ran.

Outside the office, I found myself in a narrow prison hallway. Pained moans and screams emanated from every cell I passed. These girls didn't sound as docile as the queen and her ass had suggested.

At the end of the hall, I came to a staircase exit. Walls of climbing lava blocked the route down. I could only go to the roof. I took the steps three at time.

Outside, clouds waited.

It was easy to see the reality behind this 6S illusion. An expensive cathouse in a dangerous slum would station air taxis on its roof, sparing rich customers the need to travel through the hellish neighborhood below.

I stepped onto a cloud and sat next to a harp. "Tribeca," I ordered.

Nothing happened. Was I wrong about air taxis? Or did my hallucinatory speech not communicate my destination?

I banged my lobster on the harp.

Of course, nothing happened. I kept money on my watch, not my phone.

The roof's staircase door opened. The Doberman darted out, followed by Eunuch and two Satans. I pointed my gun. A Satan fired first. It hit the cloud. The cloud lifted off the roof. I checked my lobster. The blue blood clot shrank. The taxi was going the wrong way.

In a panic, I pounded my paw on the harp and yelled, "Tribeca, Tribeca." The pad of my paw cracked, dripping blood along the harp's strings. The cloud spun around.

The growing blue embolism on my lobster confirmed: we were going toward my watch.

I was getting good at decoding my visions. Hit by a gun, the taxi had taken off to protect the owner's property, heading back to base with me on board. The harp was a fare collector. When I'd banged my paw on it, the taxi got a scrape of DNA from my hand and used it to draw the fare from my account. Now it was taking me where I wanted to go.

On the way to Tribeca, my reality whited out into a heavenly glow. When I came out of it, the campy, cheap colors of my experience had gone white on white. I regained human form. Almost. Wings sprouted from my back. A halo rose over my head. I wore a robe. Nauseating harp music filled the sky.

How many times did I have to die tonight?

GETTING CLOSER

My cloud, or air taxi, set down beside a canal. The odd man-made tributary flowed in two directions: to the Hudson River on my right and the Centre Street Dam on my left. Black-and-white film vision returned, clarifying the canal's traffic. Sharks, motorboats, rag-clad mannequins, garbage skiffs, armored shipping containers, and rubber duckies defied the canal's locks to bob back and forth. I'd say everything was there but the kitchen sink, but an one floated by, a miniature mariachi inside was letting loose.

The music stunk.

None of that, though, stood out like the oldest of old New York across the canal: the thousand-year-old city of Tribeca. It flickered like an old silent movie.

Though hardly a city by today's standards, Tribeca's fifty-three sealed-off blocks still looked ominous. Castles and dwellings—tall and short, a strange mix of architectures—abutted each other to create an uneven, unruly wall. Bricks and boards sealed every door and window less than twenty feet off the ground. Every couple hundred feet or so, mounds of garbage filled gaps between castles.

One low-slung castle caught my eye. A pulsating blue light—the only color in this silent movie world—replaced the third story. The blue matched the clump in my lobster's artery.

My watch.

I twanged the harp and told it where I had to go. The cloud

59

wouldn't budge. A thought entered my mind that Tribeca was off limits to angels. Or, at least, to the clouds that transported us.

My watch was less than one hundred fifty yards away, but it could have been on Mars. No bridge crossed the canal. It was too dangerous to swim. And even if I somehow got to the other side, vicious tigers patrolled the path along the wall. They'd eat me alive if I tried to get into the city. If I was lucky. A slow claw to death was more likely.

Not how I wanted this evening to end. Not that anything tonight was going according to plan.

Speaking of plans, where were Penelope, Cheech, and Troy?

My lobster's claws clattered with the now familiar beat of demented castanets. I pushed the belly. Penelope's porcupine mouth grimaced, and the pink tip of her rat nose—now a baton with a pink pompom—oscillated.

"Devita, where are you?" she scolded. Her voice scratched my ears like an unrestored voice track in an early talking picture. "You look dead."

"That's just the robe, wings, and halo," I said. "I'm across the canal looking at the building where my watch is throwing off a glow. Where are you?"

"In the old city. Outside the building where Klecko and Cal have their lab. You've got to get here."

"How? My ride won't take me across the canal, let alone into the city."

Cheech's face took over the lobster. He still looked like a rattlesnake, but his body appeared more like a muscle-bound bouncer type with a SWAT-team neck and hard, square jaw. Like Klecko. What was 6S telling me?

"We told you the underworld was the only way in. Why didn't you get back onto that ferry like you were supposed to?"

"I had to get off. The passengers were dead, and they wanted to kill me."

"That's the 6S," said a voice near Cheech. Troy. "Let me talk to her." The fox head that replaced the snake's had greasy black hair and a pockmarked face, the look of a sly nerd. The image jiggled, as if the phone was in mangled hands. Like Cal's. Why?

"What are you near?" Troy said. "Give me some landmarks."

I told him about the raging body of water, the blocked entrances, and the blue glow from the short building that held my watch.

"Do you see a cave opening?" he said.

"Yes, but please don't send me through another portal. 6S doesn't like sudden changes of environment."

"No, this one is a cave. It tunnels under the canal and past the wall. A little hill at the other end lets you into the old city. Then it's a short walk to Klecko and Cal's lab."

"We still have to get into that building and up to the lab," I reminded him. "And take my watch from people who'll kill us first."

Penelope's head replaced Troy's. "We have a plan," she said. "A sneaky, nobody-will-see-it-coming plan." Her nose sprung out to flagpole height.

Oh My PinocchioNess. 6S presented my friends as a liar and two drug-dealing killers. Was it telling me they couldn't be trusted?

Impossible.

Friends don't double-cross Devita Duran. Not ever. Not now. And not when I'm paying them time and a half.

The angel's harp played a rich, soothing arpeggio—a warning that the fare had just crossed five hundred dollars. This night was getting very expensive.

"Get out of that air taxi," Penelope said. Her nose shrank a bit when she said *air taxi*, a real-world object. Her nose grew again as she said, "We'll be at the other side of the cave when you get out."

All night, her nose had grown. And now, when she identified the reality outside my visions, it shrunk. Were our conversations hallucinations or lies?

"Don't hang up," I said, stepping off the cloud and onto the sidewalk. "Did you just call my cloud an air taxi?"

"What about it?"

"You've been talking to my illusions all night. Sending me into caves. Telling me to trust my lobster. All night, I thought 6S was translating our conversations into hallucinations. But now, it sounds like you know where I am, what I'm seeing and doing. Why didn't you share this with me?"

Penelope's flagpole nose shrunk down to the size of a street-sign pole, then even smaller. "You couldn't handle it."

"Hey, I'm Devita Duran. I made this drug. I know what I can handle."

"No, you don't." Her nose shrunk more, down to the size of a majorette's baton.

"I'm not paying you time and a half to tell me what I can and can't handle. Nor am I paying you time and a half to lie to me."

Now the entire porcupine face shrunk.

"Don't hang up that phone," I commanded. "You're going to walk me through that tunnel and tell me what's real and what's not."

PENELOPE EXPLAINS EVERYTHING

Penelope's scowl spiked the quills on her face to attention. The antennae tangled together. A ball of brown and gray needles surrounded her beady eyes and long, pink nose.

Oh my HideousNess! Every other face Penelope had made tonight had been a makeup model compared to this one.

But I didn't need Penelope's best-of-a-poor-lot looks now. I didn't need her friendship either. I needed an employee. An obedient employee. Someone to help me see through 6S, to understand the reality outside my experience.

The cave entrance, a portal of blackness in my white-on-white world, took me to the top of a small hill. "That slope's too steep to walk," I said.

"It's a staircase," Penelope said. "You'll have no trouble steadying yourself on the way down."

"Where are you taking me?"

"A subway station." Before I could object to getting on the train, Penelope explained, "All entrances to Tribeca are closed. We're using the station's network of entrances and passages to get you across the street and past the barriers."

Penelope's nose shrank. The needles around her face relaxed. The chaotic body of water must have been Canal Street.

With each step of my descent, echoes of dripping moisture, moaning animals, and my delicate stride got louder. Putrid mineral scents got stronger, the air colder and heavier.

The brightness turned dark-on-dark. The cave's features turned purple, navy, and black. The elements washed into each other and faded out at the edges of my peripheral vision, like an old, unrestored Technicolor movie print.

This new atmosphere unfolded without the shattering of senses that had accompanied the changes of my environment all night. Was my mind was getting used to these transitions?

Probably not. I had calmed down after scolding Penelope, and for the first time tonight, walked into a cave with a sense of control. But that probably wouldn't last. The more my heart pounded, the more dramatic my transitions became.

The ground leveled off into a slick, uneven surface. Fluttering speckles and cracks of white light punctuated the near-total darkness. Some blinded me for a second or less before the cave reappeared.

The movie I'd just entered wasn't just old and faded but damaged.

I edged my way through the scene, each step oilier and more treacherous than the last.

Penelope explained, "You're walking through old rain, rat piss, and stoner blood. But that's not what it will look like to you."

A light emerged from my forehead to reveal a strange grotto. Walls of craggy, glistening rocks dripped with moisture that pooled on the slippery, uneven stone under my feet. Over my head, jagged formations above writhed and shifted, ready to collapse at any second.

"Where is that light coming from?" I said.

"You're wearing a spelunker's hat with a lamp." My porcupine employee's pink rat nose jutted.

"I didn't walk in here wearing a hat," I snapped.

"No, you didn't. 6S is amplifying your senses to render a hard-hat lamp. This illusion should get you safely through the tunnel."

I should have known this, but in the throes of 6S, I'd forgotten reality's existence. Fortunately, Penelope had stood by my side when I developed 6S. She knew how it worked. And though 6S translated our current conversations into hallucinations, I needed her guidance, even if I didn't know what she was saying.

"Why is 6S showing me a cave?" I asked.

"Because this station's deserted, dark, dank, and dangerous," Penelope said. "By showing it to you as a cave, you won't gag over the gross reality of your predicament."

Dark, dank, and dangerous? 6S shouldn't lead me to harm, but dialed up to 12:00, it could amplify delusions and suicidal tendencies.

As if she had read my mind, Penelope said, "The light is your neurosensory implant tapping into your heightened senses, giving you the vision of a safe route through the station. If 6S picks up on something dangerous, you'll see an obstacle and avoid it."

"Is the floor really this slippery?"

"You need to walk carefully here, as if you were negotiating the slick rocks of an underground stream."

Penelope's nose kept shrinking, so she wasn't lying. But still, this made no sense. "Penelope, how do you know where I am and what's here?"

"Remember when I told you to give me control of your lobster? You gave me total access, not just the coordinates from a navigation system."

"Then talk to me," I said. "Tell me about tonight. What was going on when I was outside Donlon's and all those animals poured out of fun houses?"

"End of happy hour."

"That I figured. But I was in the middle of the sidewalk, and everyone avoided me."

"You puked on two people who helped you to your feet."

"Penelope, why didn't you tell me this?"

"Devita, hallucinations are your reality. If you knew what you were doing, you would have gone mad. Or worse, headed home. Where Klecko and Cal wanted you. You'd be sitting in your apartment, too lost to create an antidote for 6S or new software for another watch. Meanwhile, they'd be hacking your invention."

The shrinking rat nose confirmed the truth in that answer.

"You know they can't crack the 6S formula," I said, finding the strength to challenger her that I didn't have at Donlon's. "Even if they spent half their Duplextacy profits, there's nothing on the market that decompile it."

"Yes, I know that, and you know that, and they suspect that. They disabled you and kept you alive as insurance."

"For what?"

"If their decompilers couldn't figure out 6S, they'd bring you to their headquarters as a slave."

"But they know nothing about 6S. They could have killed me."

"No great loss to them. They wouldn't have 6S, but neither would anyone else. Besides, Klecko and Cal could find another ambitious, unemployed STEM graduate. The government hasn't updated implants in decades. You're not the only person who sees how easy they are to hack."

Everything Penelope said made sense. "You have Klecko and Cal figured out," I said.

"You could have figured them out, too, if you weren't so high on 6S. And yourself."

High on myself? That was harsh, but true. Penelope's nose shrunk as she spoke. She was calling it as she saw it.

I kept my head down, watching my step along the slippery sandstone. The movie print whited out, stopping me. When my vision returned, a purple-and-orange-eyed pig blocked my path. It laughed as it scraped its face against a jagged edge of metal on the ground. The more it scratched its face, the more purple its eyes became.

"Why do I get the feeling this isn't the first time I went into a subway tonight?" I asked.

"Because it isn't," Penelope said, her voice direct and calm. It conveyed no worry or excitement. Nor did it tell me what to do.

She explained, "You scoff at corp. types who funnel through subway turnstiles like cows to slaughter, the faceless souls on subway trains, the tin-eyed, mush-brained robots on New York streets. Tonight, you got to be all of them. You channeled through a cattle chute to join the death-robed masses on the River Styx and came out to a world of melon-headed robots."

I climbed over the pig and continued. Penelope's nose shrunk, and the lobster's antennae once again jutted out visibly. They wiggled like whiskers on a purring cat.

Except cats are cute.

"How did I get through the turnstile?" I asked. "My money to pay fares is on my watch."

"That slaughterer was another passenger. You clopped him on the head and stunned him as he paid his fare. Then, before he could figure out what happened, you beat him through the gate."

"That's not something I would do."

"You were desperate. When a peace officer confronted you, you clopped her on the head and ran. Then you joined faceless souls on a River Styx ferry. But you weren't a faceless soul. You were a cursing, dangerous, strung-out schizoid, rubbing against a subway pole to sooth and satisfy yourself. You fell and rolled across the subway car. Someone helped you up. You grabbed his neck and choked. Nobody could break your grip."

"Until I jumped off the ferry at the next stop." The night was beginning to make sense. "Only, I didn't see a subway station; I saw a canyon. I suppose those posters on the cliffs were subway advertisements."

"Bingo!" said Penelope. "You're figuring it out. You exited the station into the no-man's-land between downtown Hell and the Midtown business districts. Then you had to walk through the ruins of the city's most burnt-out slum to get to your watch."

"And that Satan who grabbed me was a mugger?"

"Close. He was the advance man for a gang. You looked like a stoned rich girl who landed on their turf by mistake. They planned to skin you alive and use the DNA to drain your account. They sent that Satan to make sure you weren't a police decoy."

"So, how did spitting in his face stop him?"

"That wasn't spit. That was your private pepper spray, formulated by Devita Duran, the hottest mood mistress in New York. You threw your entire stash at him, saving nothing for the rest of his gang."

"No wonder my mouth was dry."

"You laid enough spray on him to trigger massive Duplextacy hysteria. You didn't need to shoot him. The pepper spray would have kept him on the ground for hours."

I remembered the two shots to two kneecaps. "I didn't need to shoot that mugger, did I?"

"No, but it's not the first time you ruined someone's life," Penelope said.

Ruined somebody's life? "What? When did I ever...?"

"You're a mood mistress," Penelope said in a harsher tone than she'd ever used with me. "You get to venues early and spread your equipment and chemicals through the area. Then, when the party or event begins, you blend in with the caterers or guests. Nobody sees you work the crowd or your misting machines."

Why was she telling me something I already knew? And why was she so down on the business that paid her salary?

Penelope continued, "If you just used happy drugs, you'd be fine. Nobody cares if they spend a party tickling tablecloths or stroking floor tiles. But your drugs make people tickle and stroke each other. Often naked. When you worked with Klecko and Cal, people would bark, bray, and neigh like animals. Now, you get everyone to fight and fuck like them. If anyone tries to stop, they get seriously and morbidly depressed."

"I want everyone to have a good time."

"And they do, but only during the party. You don't see what happens after you slip out, after the mists dissipate and the drugs wear off. You don't see how your implant hacks change people's brains, the fights and murders and suicides you provoke."

I looked at my lobster's face. If Penelope's shrinking nose was any indication, everything she said was true.

"If these parties have such bad endings, why do I command such big fees?"

Penelope said, "Who hires you? It's never a legitimate host or event manager. It's always a joker, underworld figure, or a guest with an agenda. Look at your newest client, Madam Gross. You almost become one of her kittens tonight."

I stopped and looked at Penelope and her shrinking nose. "Wait, that queen talking out of her ass..."

"Was the same customer who makes you meet with her and her advisors in a cramped toilet. The queen of the madams, who does her best thinking on the can."

"How did I get there?"

"The gang saw your pepper spray disable their buddy, so they stayed back. When they saw you had no pepper spray left, they charged. Your lobster tipped you off about a green door and the safety of a loyal customer. But behind the green door, Madam Gross saw you were stoned and needed help. She gave you a price, and you paid it."

"Are you telling me that gibberish…"

"…was your recipe for SereniTease. She doesn't have to buy it from you to control her girls anymore."

"Control them?"

"Did you really believe the persistent atmosphere you sold her was mental health medicine for prostitutes? Madam Gross caters to the sickest tastes. She needs her girls to submit willingly. Your solution was perfect. Create a drug that needs activators to work and hack the activators into the girls' implants. Then send mists non-stop through the ventilation. It makes the girls docile without affecting customers."

"She told me her girls wanted the medicine to take the edge off."

"Those weren't anti-anxiety specs she gave you. Remember those tortured cries you heard when you escaped? If 6S didn't give you a sixth sense into reality, you would have heard giggles."

"So, when she said I would be good for a lot of tuna…."

"She thought of injecting you with activators and pimping you out but decided instead to kill you. You would have died as happy as one of these pigs, but her preferred hitman liked girls who fight back."

Can you imagine wanting a friend to lie to you? Throughout her explanation, I hoped Penelope's nose would grow. But it shrank. She was telling me the scary truth I didn't want to hear.

"Why are you telling me this now?" I said. "We've worked together for years."

"I didn't put it together until tonight."

I continued my walk through the flat-colored, flickering cave. After a couple of steps, I said, "You saw everything tonight. Maybe you can tell me about those dogs."

"What dogs?"

I glanced again at my lobster, now surer that it was my phone.

Penelope's rat nose kept shrinking. The quills on her face settled into a calm, furry expression. She was telling the truth; she didn't know about the dogs.

I told her about the pit bull that tried to hump and feel me up on the way to the train. I described how a coyote set a trap for me in the canyon. The Doberman in the throne room drew a chuckle.

"How could you miss them?" I said.

"I think you were too busy dealing with them to share your phone when they attacked," she answered.

"So, you don't know who they were?"

"They could have been a lot of guys. Degenerate is the number one breed of creep in this city."

"Yeah, but what kind of degenerate wants a cursing, dangerous, strung-out schizo?"

"The kind who wants an easy target with big boobs. Especially when you use them to make a spectacle of yourself. Plenty of people noticed you tonight, not just Bick Johnstone."

Yes! I'd gotten Bick Johnston's attention!

But wait! I never told Penelope about Bick Johnstone. Or maybe I did and 6S hallucinated that conversation into something else.

"The man with the hottest plunger on the planet noticed me. Maybe Donlon's wasn't a bust."

"No, but your life is."

"My life?"

"Yes. You're in trouble, and not just with Klecko and Cal. Their low-key mood mistressing business flew under the cops' radar for years. But you wanted to make it into an art. They gave you those three months figuring you'd overdo it and get busted."

"The cops haven't caught me yet."

"No, but they know about you, and they're closing in. Cheech and Troy got rid of them at your last event. But now they know your tricks. They'll grab you at your next gig."

Her nose didn't grow. Penelope was telling the truth, but her judgement seemed off. "Since when does the law care about a bunch of stoners at a party?" I asked.

"They don't care if people get stoned. They care how," Penelope said. "Our brain implants belong to Amerika United, not us. Every time you hack one, you tamper with government property."

"Sounds like a misdemeanor charge."

"How many parties have you done? How many implants have you hacked? One event gives them enough counts to put you away for life. No shot at parole until your boobs droop past your belly button."

Sadly, Penelope's nose shrunk again. She was now the same little porcupine with the same little rat nose who'd first showed up on my lobster at Donlon's.

Still ugly.

"What about tonight? 'Twist the lobster's tail into my face.' 'That blue blood clot moving through the main artery is your watch.' 'Go into the cave.' How did you know what I was seeing and hearing? How did you direct me through these hallucinations?"

"I can't answer that question," Penelope said.

"Can't or won't?" I pressed.

"I just knew."

No Pinocchio. No sign of lying or misdirection. Just like I knew I wasn't in a cave but accepted these hallucinations for guidance, I took Penelope's answer at porcupine-face value.

And right now, that value was huge. Penelope was proving to be more friend than employee. She made me see I had to go straight even though it might cost her job. But I wouldn't let that happen. I'd pay Penelope's salary until I—no, *we*—figured out another way to use my talents for profit. And I'd employ her in whatever new—and legal— venture I pursued.

Distracted by these thoughts, I stepped on a rock. It grew a tail and legs and darted out from under my foot, throwing me off balance. I grabbed a stalactite to break my fall, but it cracked off the roof of the cave. It looked like another goodbye-kneecap moment, but for the second time tonight, I landed on a stoned lump of flesh. Another masochistic sow. Its lifelike appearance and pink color defied the old-movie darkness of the tunnel. With hearty giggles, it had gnawed through its belly and intestines to play with its feces.

"You couldn't warn me about the rat," I said to Penelope.

"You didn't look down. You need some awareness for 6S to

work." Her nose stayed small and calm.

The sow let out a lazy, wallowing squeal. I got to my feet. The pig studied me with the same purple eyes I'd been seeing all night. Purple with flecks of orange. Had these tiny spots been in the eyes of all the pigs I'd seen tonight? Had I been too high or hurried to notice?

I continued through the cave, stepping over and around many pigs on my path through the grotto.

"What's with their eyes?" I said to Penelope.

"Duplextacy. These big, barely breathing lard piles are strung out on your invention."

"Can't be," I countered. "These creatures are drug addicts. Duplextacy's not addictive."

"Klecko and Cal tweaked it. Remember?"

I was nearing the end of the cave before the implication hit me. "Oh My Morphing MorphineNess!" I shouted. "Klecko and Cal didn't tweak Duplextacy. They added an opiate to it. How brilliantly evil!"

Penelope's head tilted. Her quills bristled. One formed a question mark.

"The opiate dulls the pain," I explained, "so neurosurfers need more pain to get high. Meanwhile, the opiate addicts them. The more Duplextacy they take, the more pain and Duplextacy they need. They take more and more until…."

Penelope nodded. "Sure, you mocked the feeds that coined *Death by Duplextacy*. You said they had the wrong drug. But you can be proud, Devita. You're behind the epidemic of homeless stoners torturing themselves to death all across Amerika."

Oh My Dirty HandsNess! What have I been doing with my life?

I reached the small hill at the other end of the grotto. As I climbed it, the weight and light from my spelunker's hat faded. "If Klecko and Cal can turn Duplextacy into a gold mine of death, what can they do with 6S?"

"Only they know. But whatever it is, *you* have to stop them."

"I have to stop them?" I looked at my lobster. Penelope's face became smaller and scrunchier. "What about you and Cheech and Troy and the time and a half I'm paying you?"

Penelope ignored the question. "Come up that hill," she said.

At the word "hill," her nose grew. Of course it would. That hill was stairs. I watched my lobster as I climbed. Penelope's face crumpled like a wet tissue. Her nose grew. I said, "Didn't you say that you were waiting for me outside Klecko and Cal's lab? That we'd go in there together?"

"Step outside that cave, and you'll be in Tribeca." Only Penelope's rat nose remained. Her porcupine mouth had sucked and swallowed the rest of her face. Even the antennae had disappeared by the time I reached the hilltop. "I'll be there when you come through the gate."

All that remained of Penelope was her nose, the longest nose with the reddest red tip of the night. It could have been a missile or a rocket. But lobster's mouth had no problem swallowing the nose before the porcupine face completely disappeared. Penelope had disconnected.

I left the cave and stepped into the bleached-out darkness of night.

Above me, the Tribeca gate loomed. The spiked iron latticework would drop on anyone who didn't belong in the city. Fresh bloodstains on the spikes told me the gatekeepers had been busy.

6S transformed my worn, faded, scratchy old Technicolor movie print into a pre-digital television screen. One with poor reception. Static and hissing obscured the ancient city's torch-lit square and the castles, built edge-to-edge, that formed most of the wall. Lions and tigers patrolled the cobblestone and dirt streets. Where the roads ended, heaps of scrap metal, garbage, and carcasses sealed the city off from the rest of New York. Tribeca's walls and heaps of trash—human and otherwise—kept residents in, not just outsiders out.

Down an alley to my right, about a block away, the static cleared up to reveal a blue glow. It emanated from a narrow archer's window on the top story of a low-slung castle. My watch.

"Penelope," I shouted.

No response.

I checked my lobster. The blue blood clot had taken over the belly, which now displayed no evidence of a black dot. I pressed the area where it should have been. The lobster's face remained a lobster.

Its antennae wiggled and looked me in the eye.

"Call Penelope," I said.

The snowy static distorted the lobster's face. Were strands of brown hair replacing the antennae? Why did they spread across the top of the lobster's head? It didn't seem right. I knew Penelope didn't have a head of quills, but was her hair brown? How could I not remember?

Through the static, the lobster's beady, black eyes morphed into blue irises embedded in drawn, angular folds of skin. Oddly familiar but matching no mental picture I had of Penelope.

Shapeless honey rose lips and an unnaturally straight nose replaced the lobster's alien features. The shell around the lobster's mouth harshened into a blotchy human jawline that reached too high, past sunken cheeks to arrive at harsh cheekbones. A small but glaring, red, figure-eight splotch stood out below the right eye.

The static dissipated, and brown hair grew to the shoulders, framing the unsightly excuse for a human face. "That's not Penelope," I almost shouted. "That's—"

Wait! I didn't know any Penelope. Coyne or otherwise. Cheech and Troy weren't human bouncers. They were names I'd given the chemicals I misted to keep angry stoners from turning their violence on me.

I looked again at the face that answered my call. The face that used to be a lying, scheming, rat-nosed porcupine. The face that belonged to....

Oh My Raving RorschachNess! Penelope was me. My unconscious self.

What did this mean? That I had no friends or employees? I knew that. That I had a death wish? I could accept that. That I was the abominably grotesque blend of two rodents?

Was I that ugly?

And wait! There are no thousand-year-old walled cities in New York. 6S had created that memory just like it had created Penelope.

I was in Anarchia.

ANARCHIA

Before the feeds branded it Anarchia, this little patch of Manhattan was *Tribeca*. The coolest, richest, most expensive zip code in New York. That ended with the Gucci Riots. Gangs of the unfashionable and under-accessorized overran the area. They evicted or killed the elites and looted everything worth anything. Jewelry, furniture, cars, tempered glass windows—if it had value, they took it.

Once they owned the neighborhood, the rioters organized a gang called the Psychocats. Allegedly to keep the peace. In reality, the Psychocat masters used their newfound sovereignty for profit.

Gang members combed streets of New York, rounding up thousands of homeless druggies and schizos and dragging them into Tribeca apartments. Media feeds cheered the redistribution of wealth. Nobody dared report that Psychocats warehoused their new tenants ten to a room and stole their government welfare payments.

As for the real warehouses, the one-time industrial spaces that New York developers turned into luxury apartments—Psychocats reverted them to their original purposes. Sort of. Anarchia became a manufacturing and distribution hub for illicit industries. It now supplies most of New York's illegal drugs plus untaxed booze, cigarettes, coffee, perfume, cookies, art supplies, candy, medicine, and garden vegetables.

Their tomatoes are the best.

Anarchia is also the deadliest, most closed-off, self-governing district in Amerika.

On the first two stories of buildings along the border, bricks and concrete seal every window and door facing out. Giant heaps of collapsed building remnants, looted furniture, and human body parts seal the streets from the outside world. Subway tunnels are the only way in and out of the area.

Under the influence of 6S, the crumbling remnants of Tribeca became a torch-lit, battered relic of a once-great medieval city. Flickering flames from grimy, cracked stone dwellings threw a jaundiced light on the jagged, overturned, carcass-littered square.

No static. No movie sets or film effects. The medieval city hallucination expressed itself as reality. A horrid reality.

Patrolling tigers shed muddy shadows on the bloody, shredded remains of wolves, pigs, cats, and...Oh My UdderNess, cows.

Once again, I had become one. I felt the tugging at my teats.

I didn't know why Penelope insisted I not go back to my apartment to create an antidote or watch hack. Fantasies of stringing her by the toes and cutting off her Pinocchio-rat nose went through my mind.

Then I remembered she was me. Something in my subconscious knew I needed to be here. I had to pull myself together and get through this without the help of an imaginary friend.

This wasn't the first time my business took me to dangerous areas. First rule: if you stood tall and walked like you belonged, nobody bothered you.

I stood on my hind legs. The impossible hooves at the ends of my forelegs grew fingers. My lobster remained in my right hoof. It pointed me in the same direction as the tug on my teats: up a narrow alley and to a three-story building. A blue glow on the top floor said my watch was within reach.

I copped my best Don't-mess-with-Devita-Duran posture—or, at least, the best imitation of it I could do as a cow—and strode confidently toward my destination. Maybe the first time in history a girl walked three steps through Anarchia without killing someone or getting killed.

But three steps was as far as I got.

Two tigers, also on their hind legs and holding crowbars in their paws, blocked my path. One swung his crowbar back and forth like a pendulum. The other tapped his into an open paw. They both growled.

Anarchia, I should have remembered, isn't like other dangerous neighborhoods. The Psychocats won't let you live, do business or pass through until they see you kill someone, even one of their own. Most first-timers come through the subway shooting. Others drag a victim through the subway and murder them in the square.

I had done neither, and this looked like my last chance.

I drew my gun. A crowbar from a third tiger standing to the side knocked it to the ground. Without a gun, I didn't have a frog's chance in a French kitchen of getting to my watch alive.

I turned back toward the Tribeca gate. Another crowbar-wielding tiger blocked that path. A baseball bat protruded from between this one's back legs.

I was sure attracting a lot of tumescence tonight.

"Looks like you got off at the wrong station, Little Red Calendar Cow," the bat-boned Psychocat said.

Or, at least, that was what I heard. As I'd learned from my experience with Penelope—actually, myself—6S translated exaggerated stimuli and responses into hallucinations yet kept my thinking intact. I was sane; I just didn't know what I was seeing, saying, hearing, and doing.

I stepped to the side so all four Psychocats could see my face, but I looked at the beta cats. "You're going to stand there and watch like puppies while this guy takes me?" I said.

Cats hate to be called dogs. *Puppy* is a huge insult.

"You won't even get sloppy seconds," I continued. "He'll kill me before you get a turn."

The tigers looked at each other. I had them. Dogs, by instinct, obey the rules of the pack. Cats, like these tigers, are territorial loners. Fear, greed, and violence held this group together.

"This night will end like every other," I continued. "He gets the tuna. You get nothing."

Again, the beta cats exchanged glances, then turned to their bat-wielding leader. Judging by his evil smile, he wouldn't sway.

77

"I have four bullets left in that gun on the ground. I could have killed one of you coming through the gate, but I was saving them for some guys. Guys who have something you want."

If I didn't say that, whatever I did say was close. These tigers would have ripped me apart if I'd babbled hallucinogenic drivel. Regardless of what actually came out of my mouth, I'd gotten their attention.

I brought my voice down to a conspiratorial notch. "Come with me, and I'll see that you get a million dollars' worth of Duplextacy each." I turned to the horny batter, the alpha cat. "Including you."

"You're bluffing," the alpha said. His voice, too, quieted slightly.

I lowered my voice even more. Lots of Psychocats patrolled this area, and if others heard this conversation, negotiations would get hairy. And not in any waxable, shaveable, silky-smooth-out-able kind of way.

"I can take you to the lab where they make Duplextacy," I added. "You know it's in Anarchia. Where else would it be?"

They said nothing, but their stares and head shakes suggested curiosity and confusion.

The leader said, "How do you know where the Duplextacy lab is?"

I showed them the belly of my lobster and pointed to the blue blood clot. "It's right here."

Four puzzled Psychocats looked at each other and back to me. "Give me that lobster," the leader said.

"Why, are you hungry?"

One of the underlings pulled the lobster from my hand.

The Psychocat's eyes furrowed at the lobster's belly. The leader squinted at it.

Of course, they couldn't read the navigation system. Like every device in my illegal life, my lobster needed contact with my DNA to work.

"It's my lobster," I said. "The navigation only works in my hand."

I didn't need the lobster to get to my watch. The blue glow up the alley told me where to go. But I needed Psychocat protection to get there.

They glared at me and bared their sharpest teeth.

"Look, you guys think I'm stoned and crazy. You're right that I'm stoned, but I'm not crazy. I can take you to the Duplextacy lab. We can take the owners by surprise. I'll kill them to earn my right of passage. Then I'll leave you with the lab. The monopoly on Duplextacy can be yours."

No response.

"You think your bosses won't approve? Your bosses only care about their take. They don't care who pays it. I'll make sure you get the lab, the supplies and equipment. The Duplextacy monopoly will be yours."

The leader pushed his crowbar in my face. "What good is the lab? We don't know how to run it."

"It's not hard to make Duplextacy," I said. "The quantum extractification and hyperbolic diffusion processes are automated."

That was a bluff, pure gibberish, but it worked. In a leadership structure so weak, the head guy has to know everything. Or act like he does.

The follower cats, the betas, looked at their leader and growled. The leader never took his eyes off me. "How do you know so much about Duplextacy?"

"I invented it."

The alpha cat dropped the bat between his legs and lowered the crowbar. So did the others. I scanned the area. Other tigers continued to patrol the area, leaving me to these four. I dropped my voice another notch. Now, we were all speaking in the same conspiratorial whisper.

"I didn't get off at the wrong station," I said. "I may look strung out, and I'm saying strange things, but I know where I am and why I'm here. I gave the Duplextacy formula to a couple of guys who double-crossed me." I nodded toward the gun. "Now I want to take them out."

Revenge. A motive Psychocats understood.

The leader spoke. "So, you take them out, and you give us the lab. I'm not buying it. You make it sound like there's nothing in it for you."

"Those guys with the Duplextacy lab drugged me. The antidote is on my wristwatch, and they stole that, too." Antidote was a simplification, but these cats didn't need to know about 6S or how it worked. "I need my watch back, and I need it tonight. Once it's on my wrist, I'll show you how to run the lab. I get away. You get Amerika's most profitable drug business."

The growling mellowed. The tigers looked at each other, then at me.

"Take us there," the leader said. "If it's the Duplextacy lab and you show us how to run it, you can take your watch and go. If not, you're gonna die a slower, grizzlier death than we had in mind when you came through that gate."

Gate meaning subway. My Penelope alter ego told me not to dwell on my hallucinations' real-life analogs. But once I got my watch back, I'd need to know where I had been if I hoped to get home.

I took my lobster back and picked my gun off the ground. Two other tigers drew guns and pointed them at me. I squeezed my gun into a sac between my stomach cage and udder. A tight fit, but not as sharp as the pinch on my ribcage. "Follow me," I said

I had no plan. But I had a better chance of getting to Klecko and Cal's lab unmolested if I traversed this dark alley accompanied by four Psychocats. That protection would end after we got into the lab and I showed them how to run it. Once they had what I promised, they'd kill me.

One problem at a time.

6S turned the journey through the alley into a shadow walk between rows of prison cells. Light here was rarer than teetotalers at Donlon's. Flickers here and there shuddered through the rusty, barred windows of the cells, leaking pukeworthy glimpses of dank walls. Lots of dead or near-dead pigs. And like all the pigs I'd seen tonight, their pink bodies and purple eyes stood out against the darkness. They curled up on spots of ground that looked greasy, slick with blood.

Occasional movie-print cracks whited out the environment to blind me. Duplextacy death was everywhere. But no image stuck like the pigs in Hell fighting to get on top of a gas-line explosion. Duplextacy death was an urge greater than sex, an urge of my invention.

We reached the castle where Klecko and Cal had their lab. The building was only twenty-five feet wide. A blue glow from the top-floor window, now bright and steady, matched the blue on my lobster's belly. My watch was up there.

Another dick-licking dog—this one a happy labrador with a tongue where its testicles should have been—guarded the castle entrance. He didn't attack or try to paw me. Seeing my tiger company, he ran off.

The tigers pulled at the door. Of course, they couldn't open it. I told them to step aside. I pressed a thumb into my lobster's throat, forcing its mouth open wide enough to fit around the lock. The door opened.

The tigers looked surprised that it worked, but I wasn't.

Security companies had stopped updating locks in Tribeca after the neighborhood fell. The takers of this building had to devise their own locking program which, of course, was no match for Devita Duran.

A creaky, crackety wooden staircase greeted us inside. The old movie-print whiteouts faded, leaving me in a black-and-white, gothic-era haunted house. My body became a Devita Duran ghost; I could see through it.

I realized that every time I died tonight, it was after an encounter with one of those dick-licking dogs?

I'd stomped on that pit bull's face and landed on the River Styx. I sidestepped a coyote and lost all corporeality. I smashed the Doberman's nose and ended up with a halo and a harp. And now, after the Psychocats scared off that labrador, the ghost of Devita Duran climbed the steps of a haunted house.

What was 6S trying to tell me?

At the first landing, I looked back. The tigers loaded their revolvers, arming for the battle ahead.

We climbed the second flight. At the third-floor landing, we came to the pearly gates.

No Saint Peter. Just a locked door with a coded entry.

Should I do this? The tigers behind me growled the inevitable answer. I squeezed my lobster's belly, put its open mouth on the locked latch. Heart bounding, I stepped into the light. A blinding totality-of-existence light.

Was this the end? Had I finally died for real?

No. Gradually, pixels of color, sound, and scents formed. My feet moved shrilly. All my senses spun back together, and when I opened my eyes....

THE LAB

Oh My Piping FlugelhornNess! A dance. A cartoon castle medieval dance.

To a chaotic blend of untuned brass, kazoo, string, and percussion instruments—music that would give mambo drums a headache—my tiger buddies and I formed a high-kicking chorus line. We faced another line of dancers: three vicious baboons—a new 6S metaphor for mob goons—led by a snake and a fox.

I'd made it to Klecko and Cal's lab.

In the bleak, dank ballroom overlaid with a morbid midnight blue haze, facelessly cruel animated beasts high-stepped toward each other and back. Toward each other and back. The dance of two brutally rendered animal packs sizing each other up for a turf war.

Our dance floor of rotting planks lay between two stone walls, one lined with a row of cluttered, dais-length banquet tables. Once-opulent green and purple banners wept from the rafters overhead, obscuring the few gray candles that flickered from the chandeliers that shrouded the ballroom in a murk of musty indigo and yellow. No wall or window marked the end of the ballroom or dance floor, just a black night sky.

Caught between this gloom and a dark place, I stood out like a barrel-chested gold robot. Which was how 6S rendered me: a robust CGI image on a flat cartoon. My dance suggested a stiff, mechanical version of my moves at Donlon's.

Klecko and Cal's dance team played the smarter fight. They guided the dance into a circle, backing my tiger buddies and me into the missing wall and the thirty-five-foot drop to the street. From this vantage, I saw a pre-digital boom box on a card table at the other end of the dance floor. On a banquet table to its left and against the wall, a blue aura leaked from a tarnished, trembling silver goblet.

Klecko and Cal had dropped my watch into a decompiler. The shaky goblet demonstrated the machine's frustration with this assignment. My original instincts were right. Klecko and Cal had no equipment that could come close to decoding my software. Next to it, a vibrating beer stein shivered like a nervous newbie dueling a master. The 6S sample inside it would crack Klecko and Cal's chemical probes before the probes could crack the chemical composition.

Past the boom box, filling the back third of the ballroom, activity in Klecko and Cal's kitchen continued without interruption. Snow White and the seven dwarfs stood on chairs and banquet tables, pulling raw ducks, onions, turnips, tarts, breads, and melons off the hanging banners and throwing them to the back wall. There, dozens of cauldrons caught the unprocessed ingredients and spit the cooked results into the air. They collided and congealed before hitting backboards and banking through basketball hoops. All kinds of mush went into those hoops, but only purple berries came out. Thousands and thousands and thousands of purple berries.

Duplextacy capsules.

Oh My UnderestimatedNess! The cash value of the lab's inventory could net my Psychocat companions fifty million dollars each if they won this rumble.

The factory, though, would be worthless. These were expendable Psychocats: not just guards, but targets for those who would shoot their way into Anarchia. The leader may have faked smarts outside, but he and his buddies knew they'd never understand this complex operation.

Which made their potential teacher, me, worthless.

Klecko and Cal's thugs danced forward. The Psychocats could back out of the missing window or go on the offensive.

The Psychocat leader, a tiger on his hind legs, wrapped his

foreleg around my waist, lifted me like a shield over his body, and raised his gun. Maybe Klecko and Cal would hold their fire if only to keep me alive for the 6S formula.

No such luck.

Klecko's venomous snake tongue sprang toward my midsection.

My robotic senses had slowed time and calculated Klecko's intention and activated my suddenly superior reflexes. I drove my heel into the Psychocat's groin. The shock weakened him enough that I could escape before the stinger struck.

I hit the dance floor rump first and rolled onto my side. My lobster lay on the ground less than a foot away. It must have fallen from my hand during the dance.

I reached for it just as the tongue, or bullet, I had dodged hit the Psychocat leader in the midsection. He fell face-down on top of my lobster, spasming, bleeding out on the floor. No point digging under his body in the middle of a gun battle. I could retrieve my lobster on the way out. If I got out.

Klecko, too, went down—for cover; he hadn't been shot. He rolled toward the wall.

I stayed low to the ground while the shooting picked up. The animals rampaged, spit, shot out tongues, and batted eyelids. One of Klecko and Cal's baboons went down, followed by another.

A second tiger hoisted me into a shield position. Deciding it better to shoot than be shot, I drew the gun from my waist and fired into his thigh. No shot went off.

The gun, taken from that Satan in Hell, must not have been fully loaded. I dropped it and repeated the groin-targeting contortion that got me out of the last shield hold. The tiger released me, and the top half of his head exploded. The bottom half of his snout caught the edge of the banquet table as he went down, suspending the lifeless torso at a thirty-degree angle from the floor.

The body slid from the table and came half-face-to-face with me. Cartoon blood spilled out from the topless skull and plumed toward my head.

I rolled away from the spreading puddle, toward the banquet table that held my watch. A baboon went down in my path. I rolled over him to my destination, a spot where two table corners met.

One table, the last in the row along the wall, had my watch. The other, a small card table, right-angled with the door. On it, the boom box blared.

The gun battle was down to two-on-two. Two tigers against a snake and a fox. The snake, Klecko, had slithered along the wall to a dead baboon that he could use for cover. The cartoon fox that was Cal had escaped into the kitchen. He hid among pots, cauldrons, and dwarfs.

Two remaining tigers, their leader dead, pulled a banner to the middle of the dance floor for cover.

I didn't move. No point going for the watch. It would give both sides of this gun battle a clear shot at this war's instigator.

Between me and the boom-box table, a box of cassette tapes rested on the floor. One tape caught my eye. If I could get that cassette into the boom box, I might get out of here alive.

A gunshot from the kitchen distracted the tigers. They fired back in the general direction of the kitchen, hitting Snow White in the eye, passing through her head, and shattering a backboard. Shards caught Sneezy in the nose, triggering a blast that knocked Dopey's ears off.

While the fox and the tigers fired at each other, I grabbed the cassette and rolled under the card table. The shooting stopped. Just for a moment. When the next round of shots started, I jumped to my feet and dropped the cassette into the boom box. I hit play and maxed out the volume.

The medieval music stopped. The tigers shrieked.

Oh My High FiveNess! I'd gotten the boom-box hallucination right: it was a portable mood mister. Not a professional device like the machines I brought to events, but good enough for Klecko and Cal to keep goons obedient and focused.

As for the cassette—nothing like a vial of fear to freak out killers, gangsters, and Psychocats.

The surviving tigers bolted from behind the banner and through the pearly gates, howling. I might have heard a dog bark but wasn't sure. I also thought I heard tumbling, but that sound was fainter, more distant.

The snake slithered up the wall and looked toward the door. The fox came out from the kitchen and pounced on the half-headed tiger. He took a bite of its neck and jumped to the other dead Psychocat. One bite wasn't enough there. He gnawed and pulled, gnawed and pulled, all to no avail.

The Klecko and Cal hallucinations glared in my direction. They would deal with me soon enough. Right now, they had other priorities. Klecko focused on the door, and Cal struggled with a chain around the whole-headed Psychocat.

Taking advantage of their distraction, I pivoted to the banquet table with the trembling goblet. I drew my watch and put it on.

Unchanged by hallucinations, this was the watch Cal had ripped off my wrist. I took a deep breath to stay calm down, grabbed the gold 6S bar, and turned it backward to twelve o'clock.

OH MY REALITYNESS

No shattering of reality. No swirling pixelated darkness or light. No misplaced sensations. Before my eyes, my medieval cartoon morphed into the dark reality of Klecko and Cal's low-budget lab. The banquet spread became a row of old, spill-stained resin utility tables, each covered with laboratory equipment and supplies.

To my immediate right, on the third and last table in the row, sat the standard software decompiler that had held my watch. Next to it was the vial of 6S Cal had flashed at Donlan's. Two probes inside it spun wildly, projecting gibberish into the air between them.

As I suspected, Klecko and Cal were trying to break my invention with cheap, old equipment. And they were getting nowhere.

Across the shadowy room, a wide-open door of dented, poorly reinforced steel replaced the pearly gates. The stone brick walls became surfaces of cracked plaster and peeling paint, the original color faded beyond detection. Chandeliers that hung from the rafters revealed as dimmed lights. The banners proved to be electromagnetically suspended barrels of neruovine, chiraloxity, opiomate and other psychoactive chemicals—Duplextacy ingredients.

One barrel lay on its side in the middle of the dance floor. Where the tigers had pulled down a banner, clusters of hard, jagged Refluxite crystals spilled out, dotting the area. Knowing Klecko and Cal, they had stocked in this synthetic salt without considering its role in biobotic engineering or figuring out that it helped Duplextacy hack implants.

The absurd convolution that Klecko and Cal had cobbled together to manufacture Duplextacy—probably on the cheap—also came into focus. Rust-streaked coils and magna pipes channeled the overhead chemicals to corroded vats, ovens, burners, reconstitutors, and recompilers. Snow White and the seven dwarfs turned out to be patched-up quantum relays and nanofluidic flows. Invisible magnetic walls created unstable channels of swirling orange and purple vapors. This decrepit assembly line further splintered into shattered tubes and spillage where the Psychocat killed Snow White. The equipment sat on cheap, biodegradable tables. At the last table, overworked recompilers sent vast quantities of surprisingly clean, consistent purple Duplextacy pills to barrels near the freight elevator on the back wall.

Through the missing north wall, now a thin layer of cheap glass, I saw the demolished ruins of New York's Hell neighborhood. The desolate stretch of decomposing skyscrapers, infernal apartment buildings, and demonic tenements extended almost a mile north.

Had I really walked several blocks in that area? And how in hell, no pun intended, did I make it?

The glass retained enough reflective gloss in the dim light for me to see my hair, now tangled and matted, framing a dirty, weary face. Dried blood, grease, vomit, piss, shit, and other New York bodily fluids speckled my bodysuit and jeans. A rip under my right breast produced a clear drop in one of my biggest assets. The smell....

No Bick Johnstone for me tonight.

On the northwest third of the apartment, the former dance floor, lay five dead bodies. One, missing half his head, lay near a row of lab tables along the east wall.

Klecko clung to the west wall, uncharacteristically rattled. Cal, also visibly unsettled, was on his knees, tugging at a dead Psychocat's neck. He twisted and curled his craggy fingers in a failing attempt to unclasp his slave tracker, the clamshell pendant Psychocat bosses use to keep tabs on their grunts.

Klecko and Cal both seemed nervous. More nervous than I'd ever seen them. Maybe they hadn't tuned their inhibitors. If so, I could set them over the edge. I pivoted back to the mood mister and lifted the box of chemical chargers—cassettes when 6S was shaping my perceptions—to the table.

Cal got the pendant off the Psychocat and stared at me, his lips pursed and angry.

"Good thinking, huh?" I chortled. "I filled the room with fear and drove those thugs away."

"Oh, you're smart," Cal snapped. "I suppose we should be forever in your stinking little debt. Two dead Psychocats." He held up the slave trackers. "If we don't hack these trackers before their bosses ping them, we'll have an army here." He stood up, twirling the chained pendant around his gnarled middle finger.

"And those two cats that got away," Cal continued, "when they tell their masters what they saw, our bribery costs will triple."

A chain slipped from Cal's finger and flew at Klecko, startling the able-handed partner more than it should have.

Klecko leaned into the wall. I'd never seen him so shaky. I took a vial of despair from the box and added it to the mood mister. Maybe if I compounded the fear....

Ssscrunchch.

The mood mister imploded, destroyed by a bizarre Planck, custom-made for the mangled three-fingered remnants of Cal's hand.

Cal pointed the photonic gun's braided filament at me.

"Stop playing games, Devita. You made it here. But you're not going to make it out if you don't do what we say."

He pointed the Planck at me and flicked it toward a ten-foot table along the wall. Starting near the window, it was the first of three lab tables, the last one being the analysis station where I'd found my watch. "Get over there," he said, "we have a job for you."

I did what anyone facing a Planck would do. I obeyed. The table had all the equipment and supplies that a psychoactive-drug test kitchen would need.

"You want me to show you how to make 6S," I said, nodding a willingness to comply.

"No, I want you to change the formula."

Near the door, Klecko chuckled. The tremor in his laugh picked up. With a blend of curiosity and fear, he inched toward the door.

"Change it?" I asked. "How? Why?"

"You think you're so smart? Start 6S at zero and charge neuridiots to get high. Our way, you start 6S at the highest setting."

"How do you make money?"

Cal chuckled and shook his head. "You just spent three hours maxed out on 6S," he said. "And you look like you almost paid with your life to get back to normal. How much would you have paid in cash?"

Oh My Fleecing FormulaNess! I knew Klecko and Cal were tough guys. Bad people. But this was TOO EVIL.

Cal continued, "Your way, neuridiots pay weekend nights to get high. Our way, they pay us every day to function. Now get to work."

A swivel stool squatted between the table and the back wall. I circled past the window, sat down, and sized up the materials. Cal wasn't entirely off when he'd bragged about their upped lab game. Fifty base compounds. Quantum recompilers to blend them at the subatomic level. Hensen burners to scorch off any unwanted quarks, atoms, and molecules.

It all looked old and used, but functional. I could make anything short of atomic fuel here. I reached for a beaker.

"Not that one," Cal said.

Uh oh. Klecko and Cal had documentation beakers. They log every compound that goes into them, along with every recompiler operation. No masking your inputs here. In theory, these beakers can spit out step-by-step instructions to replicate any formula that's produced in them.

Still, Klecko and Cal, with their bean-counting priorities, had purchased old, almost obsolete models. I could baffle these beakers. I could destroy their 6S sample, leave them with a trail of doc rot and no useful output. Klecko and Cal wouldn't know what I'd done until they tried to build an assembly line. By then, I'd be out of there. Or dead. Either way, I would foil their plan.

I threw classic ingredients into the beaker: lysergic acid diethylamide, phencyclidine, methylenedioxymethamphetamine. Though I'd never again turn a church service into an orgy, this was not the time to forego my illicit skills.

Klecko, meanwhile, reached the open door. It opened inward.

"What are you doing?" Cal said.

Perfect. A distraction. While Cal looked toward the door, I dropped two recompiler probes into a documentation beaker that could barely follow one. I programmed them to contradict and counteract each other.

Klecko said, "I think there may be something out there. I heard *ssscrunchches* when those Psychocats ran out."

Wait! The dog barks! Planck bursts themselves are silent, but imploding targets have a distinctive sound.

"I didn't hear anything," Cal said.

Of course, Cal hadn't heard. He was in the noisy factory when I turned up the fear. But Klecko, at the east wall, would have heard imploding flesh through the open door.

"I want to make sure there's nothing out there," Klecko said.

"Okay, but make it quick," Cal said. "And close the door when you get back."

Klecko looked out the door. *Ssscrunchch.* His head imploded.

Cal turned his head toward the door. *Ssscrunchch.* Cal's neck turned in on itself, spitting out blood and spine like a blown pressure valve.

Cal's head rolled off his body toward the door. His torso fell toward the open quarter of the room that had been the dance floor, the area now littered with dead bodies.

Somebody wanted blood. I expected a Psychocat to come through the door and shoot me next. But at the door appeared...

"Creepo Manchuo?!?!"

LITTLE LORD LOLLYGAG

Oh My SleazeNess. The guy who'd hit on me at Donlon's was at the door with a Planck. Klecko's headless body lay at his feet. Cal's lay near the imploded mood mister about ten feet in. And now their killer had a clear shot at me.

"Creepo Manchuo," he said, his voice an angry pant—every bit as slimy as it sounded at Donlon's but now slowed by exhaustion and breathlessness. "That's one name you haven't called me tonight."

"Not to your face," I meant to think that to myself, but it came out in a nervous mutter.

His trip here had been at least as rough as mine. His black shirt, shredded, revealed an open-sored, chemically burnt splotch on his oily, rust-haired chest. Ooze from a similar burn on his cheek weighted a side of his orange mustache so it pointed down. The other pointed up to a broken, swollen nose and shiner. His lips and chin were shredded like they'd been stomped on by a....

Oh My Plot ThickensNess. Creepo Manchuo was the dog who pawed my teats on the way to the slaughterhouse. Or, if I wanted to face reality, the perv who copped a feel outside the subway.

I thought I'd left him in the chute. Actually, the turnstile line. How did he follow me here?

"You like to make up names, don't you? Little Lord Lollygag. Mister Goo Suck. Harry the Hydrant Humper."

So that's what those moo-moos, beep-beeps and mew-mews had

meant. "All those dogs were you?" My surprise overwhelmed my ability to keep quiet.

"Dogs? Another name? Maybe you should call me what the feeds call me."

"You're famous?"

"No, their name for me is. I'm the Thursday Night Strangler."

"It's only Wednesday."

Even without 6S, this made no sense.

Still panting, he stole a deep breath and pointed the Planck in my direction. "That's what they call me, not what I am." Trampling over Klecko's headless corpse, he stepped into the loft and closed the door. "The thirteen bodies they found Friday mornings are the girls they know about."

Ssscrunchch. I glanced over my shoulder. The wall's implosion smoldered a quarter inch wide of my right ear. He chuckled and fired again. *Ssscrunchch.* The wall on my other side imploded. The burst had missed my left ear by the same narrow margin.

Another chuckle. His panting eased, and a slimy venom spread into his voice. "I'm not going to blow your head off. Of all the girls I've killed, I'm going to make your death the slowest and most painful yet."

I understood why he would want that. Never mind my cow stomps to his face. 6S had helped me spot him among the Duplextacy addicts in the subway and sidestep his charge. Oozing sores matched the spots where the coyote had hit the glue trap set for me. He could also blame me for the shiner and broken nose. They lined up with the spot where I'd slammed the door on the Doberman at Madam Gross's.

No wonder 6S fed me death imagery after every encounter with a dick-licking dog. Every time I'd gotten away from him, he recommitted to killing me.

But how had he known where I was each time he'd found me? Including now?

The battered creep stepped into the room and angled toward the lab table where I sat. A few steps in, he soccer-kicked Cal's fallen head into the window. The head was heavy for the kick. It fell to floor just short of the cheap glass.

Creepo Manchuo stepped over Cal's limp body and closed in. He dropped his Planck-holding hand to his side. *Thursday Night* may have been off, but when it came to women, the *Strangler* part of his moniker hit dead on.

Bodies of fallen thugs and the lab table lay between him and me.

I dropped more chemicals into the beaker and activated the catalysts. A display between the handles read seventeen cycles—twenty-four minutes and twelve seconds to complete the operation. No way I could hold him off for so long.

I rose from the chair and sidled along the wall toward the back of the room. I got past the lab table. My would-be killer stood his ground. Slowly craning his neck, he watched me pass the second lab table to the third, the analysis station.

Redundant gibberish continued to stream between the decompiler probes my old bosses had stuck into 6S. The vial might have held countless clues to its origin; I couldn't leave it behind. In a calculated risk that Creepo was out of position to shoot, I pulled the probes and took the vial.

Creepo Manchuo twisted his body and stared. The gun stayed at his side.

I moved the vial to my inside-thigh pocket and continued along the wall. Knowing he could charge any second, I kept a table between him and me.

Creepo stood still, straining his neck to keep me in sight. His breathing devolved into a feeble series of gasps and chokes.

Once I was past the analysis table, I turned, advancing behind the shattered mood mister and toward the door. His body stiffened. Twisting his waist to see me, beads of sweat rolled down his temple. For some reason, his feet shuffled, searching for balance. His hands twitched with the unease of trapped prey.

Oh My Lucky StarsNess! Once again, I'd drawn an inside straight in tonight's poker game with death. The fear mist that had driven out the Psychocats still hung in the air. The Thursday Night Strangler was frozen in place.

I had a clear path to the door, and Creepo Manchuo made no move to stop me.

I walked faster toward the door, abandoning the buffer of a table. Only a couple of dead bodies lay between a frozen psycho killer and me.

Halfway to the door, Creepo Manchuo charged.

Oh My What Was I ThinkingNess! I'd played the chemicals, not the man. Psychopathic killers channel fear into violent rage.

I raced to the door.

But wait! I couldn't go out there.

I had no Planck, no rep for brutality. Unless I killed a Psychocat or two, I'd never get to the subway alive. Plenty of Plancks littered the floor. Could I get to one before Creepo Manchuo got to me? He had anger and strength. I had streetfighter training. I could turn his charging rage against him.

The killer got within a foot of me and reached for my throat. I ducked under his legs and came up, flipping him. As he came down, I grabbed and twisted his wrist midair. The Planck fell from his hand. He landed with a plop atop one of Klecko and Cal's dead goons.

This was second time I'd flipped him tonight. And like the last time, he wouldn't stay down long.

A light switch on the wall, just past Klecko's body, caught my eye. If I killed what little light came from the overheads, he'd be blind. But I could use 6S to see. Set low, say two o'clock, I wouldn't need a non-existent Penelope to navigate the hallucination.

I got to the light switch. Creepo Manchuo sprang at me. I hit the switch and in the same motion rolled along the wall to escape his assault. His momentum brought him into the wall.

I didn't need 6S to see his boiling rage.

The switch didn't kill the lights. Instead, it maxed out the luminous overheads, bathing the whole room in bright light. Light enough to turn the full-wall window into a huge mirror, doubling every horror before me. Two dead Cals. Two dead Kleckos. More dead Psychocats and goons than I could count. And on the floor near the window, two severed Cal heads stared at each other with the grotesque, frozen, wide-eyed realization of bloody, lifeless horror.

I sprang from the wall and ran toward the table where my recompilers cranked away. Creepo Manchuo also jumped from the wall. He was faster. He grabbed my bodysuit from behind, spun me around, and threw me to the floor.

Never mind the kneecaps, this would have been a goodbye-spine moment if my back didn't land on Cal's lifeless torso. A double goodbye-spine moment. Creepo Manchuo dived on top of me, landing his left forearm on my ample chest, pinning me against the cadaver.

He wrapped his right hand around my hair and pulled my head back. His left forearm edged toward my throat.

"You shouldn't have thrown that drink in my face." His voice quaked. Down close to the floor, the fear mist settling from the air was stronger. Not strong enough to conquer his murderous rage, but strong enough that he had to talk through his mixed feelings of fear and anger. If I kept him talking, I could buy myself a few seconds to escape.

"I told you I didn't want to drink with you."

"That's not what you said," he wheezed. "You said that you'd have a drink with me if I served booze at my wake."

"That offer still stands," I said. "In fact, I'll make it a promise." I was nervous, saying out loud every thought I had.

He released my hair and brought his hand to my jean's waistband.

"Very funny," he snarked, tugging at my jeans.

His eyes closed. His face reddened. He clenched his teeth. His breathing shallowed and sped up.

Oh My PrematureNess. He was coming. And not a moment too soon. For me, that is. It gave me a couple of precious seconds of orgasmic weakness.

But for him, it was way too soon. He leaned his frustration into my neck. Against the wall or floor, he might have cut off my airways like he had those of thirteen women in thirteen weeks. That we know of. But atop the unevenness of Cal's small, limp, decapitated form, I could shift my head, sliding his forearm from my trachea to a neck muscle.

So positioned, I could breathe.

I could also take advantage of Creepo's sexual and psychic distraction.

I picked a spiked Refluxite crystal off the ground and smashed it into the oozing sore on his face. The synthetic salt added an intense burning pain to his fear and anger.

He opened his mouth to catch his breath. I shoved the hard, spiked crystal down his throat. The orgasmic breathing turned into a convulsive gag, weakening him enough for me to roll out from under him and away from Cal's body.

I jumped to my feet and darted to the lab table, hurdling dead bodies on the way.

At the table I checked the recompiler. It had completed two cycles but needed to complete fifteen more—nineteen additional minutes—to finish the process.

Creepo Manchuo got to his feet and spit out the crystal. Barreling toward me, he was clearly no longer affected by the fear mist.

Anger and pain drove him now. And I didn't know if or how my unfinished compound could affect him.

I ripped the beaker from the recompiler. He got to within three feet of me, and I threw the contents in his face.

A swirling mist of who knows what engulfed us. The mist wouldn't affect me. I only used chemicals that my hacked implants inhibited. But at that concentration, the chemicals made Creepo Manchuo's throat burn and eyes water. He continued toward me in a heavy rage.

Reaching back, I swept the lightweight lab equipment off the table and into his eyes.

That seemed to shunt the anger and pain to the side of his consciousness. Creepo Manchuo stopped and his face cycled robotically through smiles, frowns, dazes, and stares, each expression more exaggerated than the next.

In what state of mind would he settle? Would he be anxious or calm? Delirious or lucid? Desperate or composed? Was he going to land angry, sad, delighted…? Would he laugh, scream, cry…?

Yes, I'd be more careful this time to work the man, not the drug. But it would help to know how the drug affected him. And when it would kick in.

I stepped out of his field of vision and positioned myself behind him to his left. Plenty of Plancks littered the floor amongst the dead goons and Psychocats. If I got out the door with a couple of guns, I could get out of Anarchia.

But I wasn't going anywhere until I neutralized the threat in front of me.

Creepo Manchuo had his back to me. In the mirrored window, I saw more confusion cycling into his uncertain, ever-changing expressions.

A Planck next to the half-headed Psychocat lay about six feet in front of me. It might as well have been a mile. At any moment, Creepo Manchuo could get his bearings and beat me to it.

His eyes, squinting and tired, met mine and froze in place. His facial expressions cycled more spasmodically.

I returned his eye contact and smiled. "Hi, there," I said.

His eyes widened. His mouth gaped. I didn't know how much time I had before his psyche came to terms with the drug and he thundered toward me.

"Don't look so puzzled," I continued. "Those chemicals knocked your implants out of whack. That's why you see me in front of you while my voice comes from behind."

I had to keep him distracted, or he'd see me move toward the gun.

I slid my fingers under my bodysuit's scoop neck and pulled it to the sides. "I know why you kill women," I said. In one simultaneous motion, I inched toward the gun—and him—and slid my bodysuit's neckline down past my shoulders.

"You walk around with lappers in your shorts. The little biobotic dick lickers keep you excited." It also explained why those dogs had tongues all over their bodies, how they'd pleasured themselves while their eyes had remained fixed on me.

I pulled my right arm through the shoulder strap and released it. With another small step, my left arm came loose.

"You pick your target. You follow her. You're always ready to go." I put my right hand under my left breast in the bodysuit and took another step. This one, less subtle. "But when you finally trap her, you go too soon. You can't finish the deed, so you finish the girl."

Carefully, so as not to scratch my boob on the underwires, I released a Himalaya.

His eyes widened and teared. The cycling of expressions slowed down, and his mouth gaped.

"Tonight, you're going to finish the deed," I said.

His head froze in a horny, confused, hypnotic trance. Drool dripped from his yawed mouth. Gaping eyes beneath furrowed brows stared back at me.

I was at the half-headed cadaver's waist, a step from the gun. Judging by the deceleration in his changing expressions, I had half a minute before he adjusted to the drug and channeled its effect to his deadly purpose.

I put my left hand under my right breast and lifted my foot but stopped mid-step. My right breast got caught on the underwire. It pinched, poised to cut me if I exposed my left breast.

"Right now, you're in a psychoactive lab with the industry's best drug designer. I can make you outlast the lappers."

I ran a finger along the underwire to the pinch. It was in the same spot that had been pinching me all night.

There, my fingers traced a tiny clamshell gripping the underwire at the bottom of my breast, the spot exposed by rips in the bodysuit. If Creepo saw me finger the clamshell, he might break out of his stupor.

I flashed my classic Devita Duran tease-of-a-wink. Not attractive in my current state, but this guy's beer goggles would turn a gargoyle into a goddess.

His leer ascended to my face.

I broadened my smile.

"You're what I call a beta dog," I said, "and I love beta dogs. I always wanted to go home with a guy like you. Give you the best body you'd never hope to touch. Show you the kind of night that makes a ten-thousand-dollar hooker blush."

While he stared at my face, I got the clamshell loose and ran a finger over its mouth. Sure enough, this was a mini tracker. When the pawing had become clawing at the slaughterhouse, Creepo Manchuo clipped it to my bodysuit. The device used my bra's underwire as an antenna.

That explained the night's tugs on my teats, actually nipples, and the pinches where my boob met my ribcage. 6S wanted me to know I was being followed, but neither me nor my Penelope alter ego got the message.

It explained why he'd stopped chasing me when I went through the turnstile. He could track me from the street. The tracer would have told him where I got off the train and that I'd stopped on the platform. While I thought I was speaking to Penelope, he set the glue-trap poster for me.

It also explained how he'd followed me to Madam Gross's. And how he'd showed up at this address ahead of me. I'd hallucinated yelling "Tribeca, Tribeca" to the air taxi, but must have given more details.

I dropped the clamshell. It landed noiselessly on the dead Psychocat. I freed an Alp to go with the Himalaya. His eyes shifted back to my bust and I stepped next to the gun. "Tonight's the night we make your dream come true." I stripped the bodysuit to my waist. "And mine."

The Thursday Night Strangler unfroze, shifting his weight from one foot to the other. His fingers twitched at his sides. The cycling expressions stopped, but his asymmetrical mustache danced fitfully as his mouth shook and his breath heaved.

The chemicals were settling in Creepo Manchuo's brain. I'd seduced him with a striptease and a promise, but he was still a psychopathic killer. I could give him everything he wanted, but I wouldn't get out alive. I had to get the gun before he realized what I was up to.

Wrapping my hands over my lowered bodysuit, I pulled it, together with my jeans and panties, down to my knees. His breathing picked up, and his eyelids fluttered. He could come at me at any second. I crouched as if to get the jeans off and....

Not good. The Planck by the dead Psychocat's head was disarmed. It must have been the one I'd dropped during my dancing robot phase.

The dead Planck left me with no Plan B. Plan A had to work.

I broke his concentration on my naked body with an exaggerated grab for the gun. That set him off. Creepo Manchuo sprang forward.

He hit my reflection in the cheap one-way glass, shattering it and hurtling through.

My unfinished mixture couldn't confuse a documentation beaker, but it was powerful enough to psych out the Thursday Night Strangler.

With a couple quick motions, I pulled my clothes back on and peered out the splintered window. The creep's broken, bloody body lay on the Canal Street sidewalk a couple of feet from the building. If he wasn't already dead, he would be before the ambulance arrived.

The sidewalk was outside the autonomous zone and a public death like this would bring police. They'd examine the body and the apartment it had flown out of—where they'd find a six-pack plus of dead bodies.

I had to get out of here. But if Penelope, aka my unconscious mind, was right, the police wanted me. I could leave no evidence that I was in this building. I checked the gold needle on my watch. As much as I was reeling from tonight's journey, I needed the sixth sense that was 6S to make sure I left nothing behind.

At 1:00, I saw little brown hairs scattered among the chaotic crime scene. At 2:00, the hairs became Devita Duran faces. They looked back at me from the light switch, the decompilers and probes, Klecko's dead hands, and the bodies of the Psychocat goons. Bigger faces looked back from documentation beakers and the top of Cal's lifeless body.

One face, almost as big as my actual head, shined through a Psychocat's limp torso, lying in the bloodiest mess on the former dance floor. Probably the tiger that had bled out.

I pulled two Hensen Burners off the factory assembly line. These selective flame throwers destroy only the chemicals they're programmed to burn off. I sucked my mirror image into the devices to program them and set the automated triggers to *Bomb*.

In seven minutes, the building would burst into flames. From outside, it would look like a massive conflagration. But instead of an all-consuming fire, it would only incinerate every strand of Devita Duran DNA in and within five feet of the building.

That included the DNA that was me.

I grabbed a backpack off a hook on the wall and loaded it with the chemicals and tools I needed to restart my lab. I also grabbed a few Duplextacy tabs. Tomorrow would be no day off. By the time I got to Donlon's tomorrow night—there was some unfinished business I had to take care of—every hospital in the Amerika United would know how to cure the addiction, courtesy of an anonymous source.

I picked Creepo Manchuo's Planck off the floor and put it in the waistband of my jeans. I also pried a Planck from Klecko's dead hand and got another from the floor next to a Psychocat.

Now fully armed, I gave the room one more scan. The Devita Duran face under the bled-out Psychocat demanded attention. A face that big indicated either tons of DNA or some non-chemical physical evidence that I was in this room.

A series of beeps interrupted that thought. Anarchia bosses were pinging the dead Psychocats' slave trackers. Failing to get a return ping, they'd open an inquiry. Which, in this autonomous zone, meant a small army of killers was on the way.

I remembered planning to retrieve something from under the Psychocat when I'd lain on the floor as a robot, but not what. And now there was no time to look.

I ran out the door and took the steps three at a time. At the bottom of the stairs, more pinging. Two dead Psychocats blocked the exit. Anarchia bosses were looking for them, too.

I remembered the barks I'd heard and the sound of tumbling— Creepo Manchuo must have killed these two Psychocats when they ran from the apartment.

I tucked the Plancks into my waistband. They pinched my narrow waist. And not in a playful, kinky, fun kind of way. Actually, it was painful as I bent over to pull the Psychocats aside.

But I couldn't move them. My street-fighting skills relied on technique, not strength. These cadavers were dead weight, as budgeable as sumo wrestlers in a food coma. The building would go up in about half a minute. And a gang of Psychocat killers would be at the door any second.

I pulled two Plancks out of my waistband and blew the hinges off the door. Nothing happened. Time to get tough. I climbed onto the dead Psychocats, balancing myself with a foot on each. I raised a leg and kicked. The door wouldn't move. I blew away the doorknob and lock and kicked again.

The door gave. It fell outward and, on the way down, caught a Psychocat on the forehead with enough force to knock him backwards onto the hard pavement. At minimum, I'd fractured his skull. More likely, he'd die of brain bleeding within a few minutes.

It looked like that dying Psychocat had led a charge. A triangle of eight more froze in place behind the spot where he fell. They gaped, stared, and expressed all forms of shock.

Behind the door that had fallen out and killed their leader, a busty girl with a Planck in each hand stood atop two more of their dead mates. I raised my gun, and the triangle of Psychocats scattered. Nobody wanted to be my next victim.

I barely got away from the building before it exploded. And what an explosion!

Stares of respect followed me up the alley and into the subway. The dirty, smelly, hot babe in tattered clothes had earned the right to come   and   go   from   Anarchia   unmolested.

THE 6S FACTOR

Twenty hours later, my watch read 8:07 p.m. on the clock and a psychically manageable 5:00 on 6S. The quiet riverbank that was Donlon's hosted only a few sparse wolves, foxes, and rats. No rabbits. At 4:00 6S, a peacock flashed his feathers at the only hen who dared come out on a Thursday night.

I'd been waiting for this. No dorkesses. Just dorks and me. I turned 6S back to a minimally enhancing 12:15 and stepped up to the bar next to Bick Johnstone. "I'm Devita," I said. "I've been waiting for a chance to talk to you."

Bick was taller than me. He looked at my face, but his eyes wandered about five inches below my chin. Those eyes were the deepest brown I'd ever seen but for a soft green sparkle in the upper right corner of the left iris.

His left. My right. The glint stood out like a firefly on a teddy bear.

"Didn't I see you last night?" he said. "You danced toward me then disappeared into that booth." He tilted his drink toward the front of the bar.

Yes! My Penelope subconsciousness was right. He'd noticed me. "I had a business meeting." Yogi set a drink down for me. Sex on the Beach, triple vodka. The big bear of a bartender knows what I like when I'm on the make.

"How did it go?"

"As well as I should have expected."

He nodded. A couple of yellow flashes interrupted the steady green glint. Was 6S telling me something?

"That must mean bad," he said. "Why didn't you come to me after your meeting?"

I tipped my glass toward him. "I didn't want to fight the crowd."

His smile broadened. A little too wide to be real. He pretended to be flattered. "So, you risked your life to meet me tonight?" The glint in his eye turned solid yellow.

"Risked my life?" This was going to be fun. I brought my voice down a conspiratorial notch. Only a few regulars dotted the bar tonight. Nobody would hear me but Johnstone. "You must be thinking about the Thursday Night Strangler. I'm not afraid of him."

Again, Johnstone sized me up. This time, though, with a more blatant consideration of my biggest assets. He brought his voice down to mirror mine. "You should be. You're his type."

"I'm a lot of guys' type, but not many are mine." With that, I flashed my classic Devita Duran tease-of-a-wink. It always makes guys want me.

Bick Johnstone, though, dropped the act. He leaned back and turned down the corners of his mouth. A red flash interrupted his eye's solid yellow gleam.

Oh, My ClairvoyanceNess! The green, yellow and red sparkles in Bick Johnstone's eye were his internal *go, caution,* and *stop* signals. I glanced around the bar. Everybody had little sparkles in their pupils. Even at its lowest setting, 6S gave me a peephole into people's minds.

Did I plan to share this power for two hundred dollars an hour? What was I thinking? I called it 6S because the hallucinations worked like a sixth sense. But 6S could also mean success.

Who needed mood misting? I could turn 6S on stock market players and clear millions. Or I could turn my love for old videos into a business and target ads with one hundred percent accuracy. I could start a STEM company and close every deal on the table.

But for now, with the law closing in, I had to lie low and limit myself to one deal. And my target's yellow caution leaned red.

"I don't know if I should be flattered or afraid for you," Bick said, his voice flat and calm, like he was doing the first read-through of a script. "You come out on a Thursday night because you want me to yourself. But being here makes you the only available target for a serial killer."

"I told you, I'm not afraid of him. When you check the feeds tomorrow, you'll see that he didn't attack me or anyone else." I spoke with only the slightest smile. Nothing flirtatious. Just a simple grin of confidence.

Bick's torso retreated. His eye still read caution. "How can you make that prediction? How do you know I'm not the Thursday Night Strangler?"

I shook my head. "Because I met him last night, and he's not you."

That got him. Bick stared at me. Actually, he stared into me. Studied me. He leaned back toward me. The yellow caution signal stood out, but no red flashed.

"Last night was Wednesday," he said. No more measured calm. This voice was a straightforward challenge.

"The feeds call him the Thursday Night Strangler. They don't know his whole story."

"And you do?"

"More than the feeds or cops. He spilled a lot of beans last night when he tried to kill me. But he was too drugged up to pull it off, so I got away."

"He was drugged up? What about you? Last night after those guys left, you sat in that booth talking to a package of Crustacies like it was a twenty-first-century smartphone."

I sipped my drink and smiled. "I'm a freelance STEM pro. You have no idea what I can do with the electrostatic properties in a tin of lobster crackers."

In truth, I could do nothing with Crustacies.

It was my business to know where Klecko and Cal had their lab. I also knew the few lock combinations Cal's mangled hands could open smoothly. 6S had tapped my unconscious mind to figure out what Klecko and Cal were up to. The drug had also created a phone and friends to convince me to stop them.

Bick Johnstone saw I wasn't being entirely truthful about my Crustacies prowess. His eyes strobed red, red, yellow, red, red, yellow, red, red.... He didn't have 6S, but he had actor training and knew how to read people. And right now, I was giving away more of myself than I could control.

"Do you expect me to believe you knew what you were doing? Last night you stumbled out of here like those guys fed you bad mescaline."

"Right idea, wrong drug," I admitted. To close this deal, I had to tell the truth. My advances had turned Bick Johnstone into a human polygraph set at *paranoid*.

In a soft, calm voice, one sure to attract no attention, I explained, "Those guys unleashed hallucinogens in my system and walked out with the antidote. It set me up for a wild night, but as you can see, I'm here now. And I'm fine."

"Yes, and during that wild night full of hallucinogens, you met the Thursday Night Strangler?" He didn't buy my story.

"After I caught up with those guys and took the antidote," I explained.

That calmed the glint in his eye a bit. More yellow than red. "You didn't hallucinate meeting him?"

"Or my getaway."

I'd seen Bick Johnstone do the curiosity act in videos, but this intrigue felt genuine. "Do you know who he is? Could you identify him?"

I nodded with no attempt to soften or exaggerate my confidence. The yellow glint in his eye flashed green. He wanted me. Enough so that even if he didn't believe me, he would play along.

"Why don't you tell the police?" he said.

"They have the evidence and their forensics. They'll put it together in a week or two." And when they do, they'll recognize his other victims and trace them back to Madam Gross. They'll find the SereneTease implant hacks in her assistant's pocket lab, and with it, a chemical formula trail to pin all my mood misting crimes on her.

Bick's voice softened even as he continued to challenge me. "Yes, but if you can stop him from hurting someone else?"

"He won't hurt anyone."

"You're sure about that?"

I nodded. "The Thursday Night Strangler won't bother me tonight. Or any night. But if it will make you feel better, you can take me home. Your place or mine. For my protection, of course."

A laugh. A real laugh. Not a faked-for-green-screen laugh. His gleam went flash crazy: yellow, green, green, yellow, green, green…. I was winning him over. "You had me going," he said. "Most girls are too intimidated to joke with me."

I smiled coyly. "I'm not joking."

A smile and a shake of his head. The green gleam in his eye solidified, but the yellow flashes popped in every few moments. "You're being presumptuous," he said. "What makes you so sure I'd go home with you? Or that I could if I wanted to? My career is at the mercy of all kinds of suits, and they've got their finger in every corner of my life. Did you see that blond lady watching my every move last night? She was my agent. She was here to make sure I went home alone."

Oh My Dream Come TrueNess! Even with all his wealth and fame, all his physical attributes and artistic skills, Bick Johnstone was a beta dog. Not a gross-me-out, only-drink-with-you-at-your-wake beta dog like Creepo Manchuo. Not a runt-of-the-litter beta dog that I dreamed of screwing just to screw with their heads. Bick Johnstone was *the* beta dog. The dog I'd wanted to mate with—I mean really mate with—when I was a cow outside Donlon's.

All interspecies kinkiness aside, the yellow sparks died out. Green light, go.

"If my agent were here tonight," Bick continued, "you'd have to go home by yourself. She couldn't care less about exposing you to the Thursday Night Strangler. Is it worth that kind of risk to score the 'Hottest Plunger on the Planet'?"

I shook my head. "Do you think I'm here because of some publicity? I know you're a green screener. Your vids are full of special effects. But I'm not some dung beetle who falls for a male that makes his poop balls look bigger. I'm here because I think there's more to you."

"Do you?" No act. No challenge. No change to the green in his eye.

"Yes, I think *Idolatry Ezine* sells you short."

Again, he laughed. The green glowed brighter. Oh My KegelNess! I was going home with Bick Johnstone. I could feel it in my—

I'll spare you the enveloping details.

But I still had to close the deal.

"I get it," I continued. "Your agent didn't let you go home with anyone last night because you had work today. But there's no shooting tomorrow, and the only things keeping you from me tonight are exhaustion and concerns about my sanity."

The green glow spread through his iris. His eye was almost completely green. No brown. No yellow.

I continued, "How about this? Let's go home together. Your place or mine. No funny stuff. You surely need rest after a week of shooting, and to be candid, I had a rough twenty-four hours, too. I bet we both can use a night off. Tomorrow morning, we'll sleep in. Then, we can go to brunch. My treat; I'm not interested in your money. After brunch, I'll show you I'm not making any of this up. I'll take you to see the Thursday Night Strangler."

A small but clear yellow dot appeared in the green.

"Are you serious?" Bick said. "The Thursday Night Strangler killed thirteen women in thirteen weeks—"

"That we know of," I added. "He killed more."

"You want me to believe that he almost killed you last night, but you got away. And tomorrow, after brunch, you're going to take me to meet him."

The yellow dimmed but remained, a reading of *questionable* on his internal lie detector. To close the deal, I had to tell the truth and I had to keep him intrigued.

Bick continued, "Why would you deliberately go to meet the most vicious serial killer—killer of women—to hit this city in more than a century?"

"I promised to have a drink with him."

The End
Thank you for reading "Devita Duran Gets Stoned"

ACKNOWLEGEMENTS

First, I want to thank Gd, my wife, kids, friends, and community for tolerating this nonsense. I'm sure they're all scratching their heads at someone who spends 45 years behind a keyboard and retires to write. Advertising paid the bills and I was blessed with a good career. But I often wondered about the comic sci-fi author I left behind.

I'd probably still be wondering if not for an email. Someone saw an early draft of Devita Duran Gets Stoned on onlinewritingworkshop.com, and sent me a personal note. He said couldn't post a review because he "was laughing too hard." Thank you. Your signed paperback copy is in the mail.

Finishing the novel proved to be a unique challenge. I wrote copy, not fiction, for 40+ years, and while there are plenty of books, YouTube videos, and podcasts (my favorites are Jim Thayer and Sylvana Gilbo), the lessons can only take you so far. Danielle Dyal, my editor, showed me what I got right, what I got wrong, and how to make what was wrong right. Thanks, Danielle. Anything in this novel that doesn't work is on me, not you.

Editing can be a nightmare for most writers. So I also want to thank every creative director, supervisor, account manager, marketing manager, strategist, client, and lawyer who critiqued my work (often brutally) over the years. I can't name all of you because there were hundreds. But every one of you made me a better writer, thinker, and problem solver.

One of those advertising colleagues, Peter, deserves a double thank you. Peter showed an early, long-lost short story to his poker buddy, Donald Westlake. The feedback was encouraging, but the story needed work. At the time, though, advertising paid the bills, and my growing family made advertising my first, second, and third writing priorities.

Donald, thanks for the boost. I'm finally doing the work.

Also by Mark Spector

Running from the Witness Protection Program:
A True Crime Confession

For the longest time, it was a family joke that Dad was in the Witness Protection Program. But when my kids started asking about it, the memories came rushing back.
Available as a Kindle eBook

ABOUT THE AUTHOR

by Devita Duran

Oh My What NerveNess! Who does Mark Spector think he is, expecting me, Devita Duran, the best psycho-pharmacist in Amerika, to write about *him*?

Mark could have made me decades ago. But noooo. Like a true beta dog, he dumped genre-bending fiction to write advertising. And now with the kids grown and out of the house, he comes keyboard crawling back.

Does Mark really think the world's waiting for his unique brand of comic sci-fi? Or that I'll write something nice after what he put me through in *Devita Duran Gets Stoned*?

I mean, really! There must be a million dorks and dorkesses writing in retirement the novels they wanted to write in their twenties.

Mark Spector is just the weirdest.

MarkSpectorWrites.com

www.ingramcontent.com/pod-product-compliance
Lightning Source LLC
Chambersburg PA
CBHW071604180626
46819CB00002B/119